D0553690

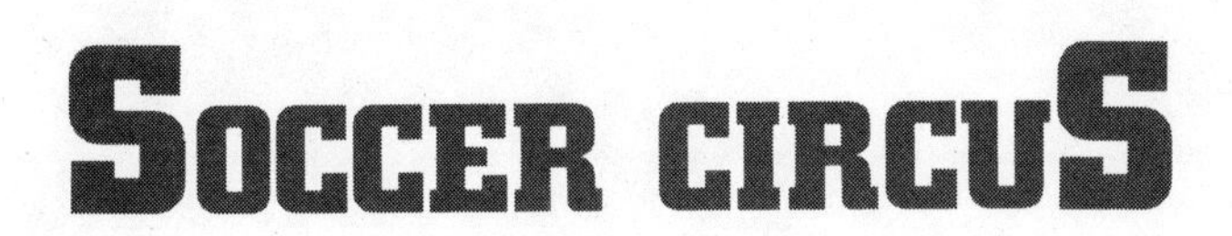
SOCCER CIRCUS

Also by Jamie Gilson

Harvey, the Beer Can King

Hello, My Name Is Scrambled Eggs

Can't Catch Me, I'm the Gingerbread Man

Do Bananas Chew Gum?

Thirteen Ways to Sink a Sub

4B Goes Wild

Hobie Hanson, You're Weird

Double Dog Dare

Hobie Hanson, Greatest Hero of the Mall

Sticks and Stones and Skeleton Bones

SOCCER

JAMIE GILSON

Illustrated by Dee deRosa

Lothrop, Lee & Shepard Books New York

Inquiries should be addressed to Lothrop, Lee & Shepard Books, a division of William Morrow & Company, Inc., 1350 Avenue of the Americas, New York, New York 10019.
Printed in the United States of America.

First Edition 1 2 3 4 5 6 7 8 9 10

Library of Congress Cataloging in Publication
Gilson, Jamie. Soccer Circus / by Jamie Gilson ; illustrated by Dee deRosa.
p. cm. Summary: In their determination to have fun while spending the night at a motel during a soccer tournament, Hobie Hanson and his friends get caught up in a mystery buff's efforts to solve a fictitious case. ISBN 0-688-12021-0 [1. Hotels, motels, etc.—Fiction. 2. Mystery and detective stories. 3. Soccer—Fiction.] I. deRosa, Dee, ill. II. Title.
PZ7.G4385H1 1993 [Fic]—dc20 92-9716 CIP AC

For Linda Lee and Robin

Welcome

Contents

SOCCER CIRCUS

1. Making Tracks

"I can't believe you did it," my dad said.

"It was dumb," I told him. "I know it was dumb, but I didn't mean to. Honest. I didn't know the cement was wet."

Dad crossed his arms and stared down at me. "The police said there was an orange sign."

This was true. I saw it later. I just wasn't looking when it happened. I was thinking about tomorrow. I was thinking about how amazing tomorrow was going to be. I was thinking trophies and banners, adventure and excitement and glory. I was not thinking about the sidewalk three doors down from my house. At all. When I rode my bike to school that morning the sidewalk was cracked and bumpy like always. When I came home from soccer practice that afternoon, it was one big, long stretch of ooze.

Of course, once I sank into the stuff I had to keep going. You can't just stop and put your feet down. You can't even back up. I had to dig right on through two squares until I got to the grass. It was wet enough to suck my tires down an inch deep. It was dry enough, though, that when I got out, my tracks stayed there like snakeprints.

I couldn't even lie and say I didn't do it. The man who'd poured the sidewalk was there. Just after I reached the grass, he ran up, grabbed my handlebars, and began to shout.

"Punk kid," he said. "Vandal," he said. "I've been breaking my back all day," he said, "tearing out old sidewalks, pouring new sidewalks, and here you come, messing it up. Two hours ago those slabs were perfect. Look at 'em now." He lifted the handlebars and bounced my front wheel up and down on the ground. "It's kids like you who give kids a bad name," he yelled.

I told him I was sorry.

"Right," he said. "Sure, sorry. Just look at those ruts! I'll have to do both squares over. Somebody's got to pay for it, and it sure isn't gonna be me."

While I stood there on the grass with my wheels practically turning to stone and my heart beating like crazy, he called the police on his mobile telephone. He kept his eye on me the whole time, too, like he thought I might to try to escape and run wild through more wet cement. I felt like one of those guys you see in the post office with two pictures, one facing front, the other sideways. I was a criminal.

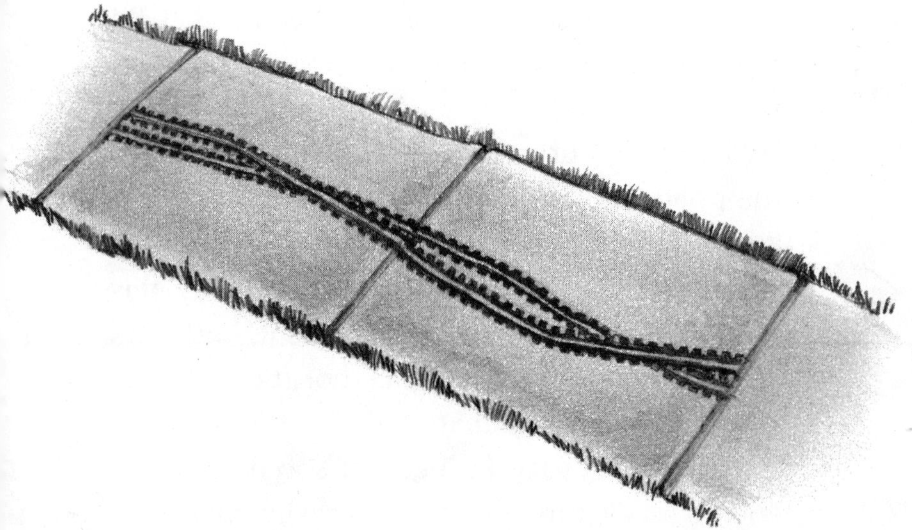

The squad car got there in three minutes flat. The policeman looked grim. He took my name. He asked me for my dad's phone number. Then he called him from the cement guy's mobile phone.

My dad works in this garage, and, it turns out, he was right in the middle of fixing a carburetor that didn't want to be fixed. He didn't want to come to the phone. He sure didn't want to hear what he heard when he got there.

After he talked to my dad, the policeman sent me home. Mom got there a half hour later. I had to tell her. She sent me to my room. When Dad came to my door after work his face was red. He was mad. I was sitting on my bed, which I'd made so nobody could say "You don't even make your bed."

"I never," Dad said, "*never* thought I'd have the police call me at work about you."

"Me neither." And that was no lie.

"What's with you?" he asked. "Already this week you blew a dentist appointment. And she's sending us a bill because it's not the first time you did. You know that."

I knew. Tuesday I'd been at soccer practice, and I'd totally forgotten to get a cavity drilled out at four o'clock. When I got to the dentist's at five-fifteen, it was too late.

"This sidewalk is going to cost us a lot," Dad went on, his face getting redder. "You heard how much?"

I'd heard. It was enough to buy two new bikes.

"And you know who has to pay?" he went on. "*I* have to pay. You are old enough to know better, but the law says I'm the one who has to come up with the cash."

There were five dollars and fourteen cents in my rocket bank. That wouldn't go far.

"You know what this means for you? This means more baby-sitting of Toby and the kids down the block so you can pay me back. This means much, much more helping your mother and me with chores. You have to learn from this."

"Yes, sir," I said. I could maybe put up a sign in the grocery store: fifth-grade criminal seeks job as baby-sitter, dog walker, or fish feeder. But who'd let their kids, or even their pit bull, sit or walk with a criminal? And at fish-feeding rates, I would have a long gray beard before I could pay him back.

"Tomorrow is Saturday," he went on, "and I'm going to be home putting in two ceiling fans. You're going to be here helping me. All day."

I took a deep breath. Maybe it was the wrong thing to say, but I had to say it. "I can't tomorrow," I told him.

"Can't!" he boomed. "What do you mean, can't!" It was the wrong thing.

"I mean," I explained, "tomorrow is the all-state soccer tournament. Remember? You signed my permission slip. And they need me. The Zappers need me. Remember?"

He didn't say yes. He didn't smile.

"It's an overnight," I reminded him. "It won't cost anything. It's free. The Park District is paying. We're staying in a motel."

"You *were* staying there. Now you're staying here."

He didn't understand. I *had* to go.

It was because I was thinking about the trip that I'd cut through the cement. At soccer practice I'd made two goals. I was thinking trophy. This was the first time the Zappers had played anywhere but the Park District field on Central Street. We weren't exactly ready for the Olympics, but we were the best team in town.

"They need me. Last year's team won this tournament," I reminded him. "Without me the Zappers would lose right away. For sure they'd lose. Then everybody would hate me." That was a *little* strong and not absolutely true, but he didn't say anything back, and he does like it that I play soccer, so I kept talking.

"Please, it wasn't like I got off my bike and wrote stuff in the cement with a stick. I didn't do anything on purpose. It was kind of like going through a red light." That was risky, reminding him about that light. But I'd been in the car when he went through one. Nothing had happened. Nobody turned a flashing blue light on him. He didn't hit anybody, but he did go through it, all right. "I didn't mean to," I told him.

"That's no excuse," he said, and he looked at me for a long time.

"I told the cement man I was sorry."

"If I let you go . . ." he began, and I knew I could start packing. "*If* I let you go, you had better be on your very best behavior the entire time you are gone."

"I will," I said. "I promise. Absolutely. Positively."

"Kids have been known to drive across wet

cement on purpose," he said, "just to see what it feels like, just to make their mark. Maybe you did and maybe you didn't."

"I didn't. Cross my heart." I crossed it. I could tell he still wasn't sure I was telling the truth.

"Have you hosed off your tires?" he asked me.

"I'll do it right now." I stood up. "Is it too late, do you think? Are they like rocks already?"

He sighed, very, very loudly. "By the way, did I see you ride through an intersection on that bike this morning with your arms crossed?"

"It's easy," I told him. "I'm a really good no-hander."

"Riding without hands makes you a sitting duck for fast cars. It's not safe. All you've got to do is *think* about it and you'll know it's not safe. That's your problem, Hobie. You don't think about what you're doing. You don't remember when you have a dentist appointment. You don't pay attention when you're on your bicycle. Listen, you get yourself into any more trouble, *any* kind of trouble, and I tell you right now some other boy who knows how to use it properly will be riding that bicycle."

"You'd *give* it away?" I asked him. What would

I do without my bike? My bike is how I move. My bike is me.

"You betcha," he said. "Or I could sell it, maybe. Guy at work has a kid who needs one."

He was backing down on the trip, but he wouldn't back down twice. I would have to be very, very careful. No more trouble.

"All right," he said, finally, "this is against my better judgement. You can go to the tournament, but only because they're counting on you. I don't want to hear about any mischief at this motel, though." He shook his finger at me. "No hijinks. You keep your nose clean, or you lose that bicycle *and* the privilege of playing soccer. You hear?"

I heard. I wanted to have a good time. He wanted me to be good. I wasn't sure they were the same thing. But, he was letting me go. Wet cement tracks and all, I was still going to the big soccer overnight. Nick, Marshall, R.X.—the whole team—we were going hours away from home. We were going to stay overnight at the Megadome Motel.

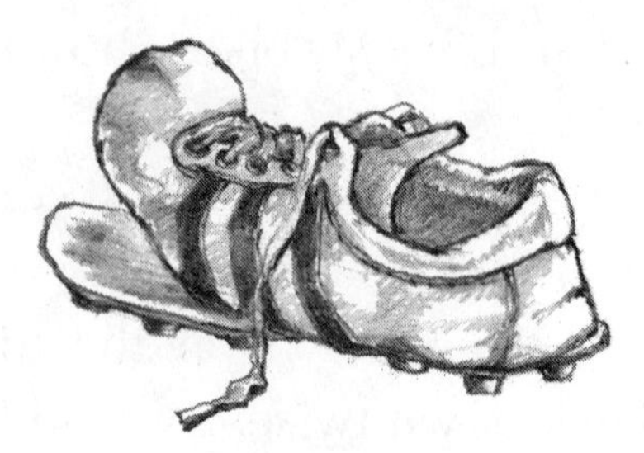

2. When Are We Going to Get There?

"Nick Rossi, you keep that shoe away from me." Lisa Soloman held her nose. "It stinks!"

"Now, boys," Mrs. Rossi called back to us. "Stop clowning around. Save your energy for the game." The car behind our minivan honked.

I wasn't clowning around. I hadn't made a single wrong move. Even my dad would say I was keeping my nose perfectly clean.

"The sole on this soccer shoe is loose," Nick called to his mom. "It's flapping like a duck." He kept wagging his foot at Lisa. "Quack."

"You cut that out," Lisa said. "You're making

it worse. That's, like, really dumb. You *need* that shoe. You can't kick a ball if it's yawning."

She slid the minivan window open and stuck her nose out. Waves of rain washed her face. Nobody would be pouring fresh cement in this weather. My tracks would still be there when I got home.

We were packed tight inside. But even sitting next to him, Lisa couldn't have smelled Nick's foot. We'd all brought sack lunches, which we'd had to eat in the van because of the rain. The place reeked of corn chips, oranges, bologna sandwiches, and peanut-butter cookies. It smelled like food, not foot.

In front of us lightning cracked the sky. Thunder rumbled like an enormous empty stomach.

"It's two feet tall," R.X. said. He was sitting in the seat behind us with Marshall and Molly.

"Nowhere near," Marshall told him. "Nowhere near two feet."

"And the soccer ball on top is pure gold," R.X. said.

"The ball is plastic. The whole thing's plastic."

"Okay," R.X. agreed, "so it's plastic gold, but it is still a very big, very shiny, very excellent trophy."

"Yes," Marshall said, "first place usually is."

"So?" Nick called back to them. "So last year's team won first. We could get a trophy if we wanted to."

Right. Sure.

Everybody stopped talking. They won last year. This year, though, we were just the best of a pretty bad lot.

"Face it," Molly Bosco said. "They're legends. They were the best ever. I don't know why we even bothered to come."

I blew my breath on the window and drew

crisscrosses on the pane for tic-tac-toe. They disappeared before I could get Nick to play.

Last year's Park District team was the Hot Shots. The Hot Shots made a big splash. Unless we were really, really lucky, we wouldn't even cause a ripple in the pond.

Nick flapped his sole at Lisa again. "Quack."

"You play in those and you'll make duck soup in all the puddles," I told him.

Nick's mother stopped at a light. "What's going on back there?" she asked. "Sounds like Old MacDonald's farm."

"Old MacDonald?" Toby asked. "I know *that* one." Toby is Nick's little brother. I baby-sit him when Nick can't. He's four. He turned around in his front-seat kid carrier and rubbed his eyes. "E-I-E-I-Ohhhhh," he sang.

He was loud. Loud is what Toby *is.* Mostly he sounds like a siren. He's practiced his whine till it's perfect. This time, though, he'd been quiet. He'd been asleep. Our trip had gone on for three long hours and Toby had slept through two and a half of them.

"Mrs. Rossi," Molly said, "I expect you know exactly what you're doing and all, but I think we've gone too far." Molly had been quiet most of the way, too. She'd told us she was writing a story for a contest, but I didn't see how she could write anything bumping up and down in a minivan. I, myself, would throw up.

"Too far?" Mrs. Rossi asked.

"Well, I could be wrong," Molly went on, "but Mr. Star said we were supposed to turn right at the Pretty Good Cafe, and there was a restaurant with that name about four blocks back. Maybe more. Of course there could be two Pretty Goods."

The light changed to green. The car behind us honked and our van jerked forward. "Are you sure?" Mrs. Rossi peered from side to side. "It's so hard to see in the rain."

I wanted to ask, I really wanted to ask, "When are we going to get there?" We'd left late. R.X.'s alarm didn't go off. But before we started, Mrs. Rossi had made us all—even Toby—line up, raise our hands, and promise we wouldn't ask. "We'll get there when we get there," she'd said.

"Are we going to get there in time?" was probably a better question. Mrs. Rossi is a very nice person, but she was driving about twenty miles under the speed limit. Kids passed us riding bicycles.

It was already after one-thirty, the game was at two, the car was creeping, and helping my dad put up ceiling fans was beginning to sound like fun. Riding in a smelly minivan with seven kids, one of them Toby and two of them girls, is not my idea of a great way to spend a Saturday.

I reached over and flipped Nick's sole with my thumb. It ripped about half an inch more. I pulled my hand back. Would my dad call that stupid?

Nick saw me flinch. "Look what you did, Hanson," he said. "You tore my shoe."

Lisa rolled her eyes.

"Mom!" he called. "Hobie ripped my shoe. Now I can't wear it for the game." Then he grinned at me. What he really wanted was black shoes like everybody else's. He'd wanted them for two months. We all had black shoes with white stripes. Nick had white shoes with black stripes. "Do you see any shoe stores on this street?"

"I can hardly see the car ahead," his mother called back. "It used to be Mr. Star's car, but we lost him miles ago, I think. Can you dig out the map that tells us where this motel is?"

"Got it right here," Nick said, pulling a crunched up envelope out of his back pocket. He took out a piece of green paper and unfolded it on his knee.

"Better still, does it say where the game is?" Mrs. Rossi asked. "I think we should go straight there. You're all in your uniforms."

"Except me," Nick said. "I don't have shoes." He ran his finger down the green page. "It doesn't say where the game is. That page isn't here. Mr. Star must have forgotten to give it to us."

"R.X.," Mrs. Rossi called, "is Mr. Star behind us?"

R.X. wiped the steam off the back window with his sleeve and leaned his head against the glass.

"There's a red sports car behind us," he said. "I think it's an Alfa Romeo. Yes, with those headlights, definitely an Alfa Romeo. Mr. Star doesn't drive one of those, does he? No, he's a teacher. Besides, Mr. Star has four kids with him. The guy who's driving is alone. He's talking on his car phone. He's got a funny, round face that's as red as his car. Interesting. He looks a little like he's going to explode. No, a *lot* like he's going to explode. It could be because we're going three miles an hour and he wants to go faster than that, but I can't be sure. He might just have high blood pressure."

"There's no car behind the hysterical guy's, Mrs. Rossi," Marshall told her. "Looks like we've ditched Mr. Star."

Behind us the horn honked very long and very loud.

"It looks from the map," Nick said to his mom, "like Molly's right. We were supposed to turn about ten blocks back."

"Where's Aretha and her dad and those other kids?" R.X. asked.

"Aretha Cabell is always on time. Mr. Cabell drove out of the parking lot at nine on the nose," Marshall told us. R.X. didn't say anything.

"I've got an idea," Molly said. "Since you guys aren't doing anything important, why don't you listen to my story. I need your input. I was going to start out, 'It was a dark and stormy morning,' but I think maybe that's been used."

"Mr. Star thinks we could win," R.X. said, ignoring her. "I think we stink."

"Winning doesn't matter," Marshall told him. "We're just supposed to go out there and have a good time. Every game Mr. Star tells us, 'I want you to go out there and have a good time.' "

"He doesn't mean it," Nick said, flapping his sole.

"I've got to go," Toby announced.

"The rest of the team is probably already there," I said.

"If my math is right," Molly told me, "and it is, that's just eight kids. You can't play soccer with eight kids. When we're late we forfeit. My grandmother will be furious." She sighed big time.

My dad would be furious, too. He'd be sure it was my fault, that I missed the game like I missed going to the dentist.

"I heard these guys we play today are the pits," R.X. said.

"The Pits?" Lisa asked. "That's a weird name for a team."

"I *need* to go," Toby yelled.

"I need a new pair of soccer shoes," Nick told his mom. "If you see a place . . ."

"Okay, win or lose," R.X. said, "what I want to know is, how many kids are going to be staying overnight at this Megadome Motel? I mean, this should be a blast."

"I heard that," Mrs. Rossi called from the front seat. "This is a sports tournament, not a blast. Last year's team was much too explosive. *You* are going to behave like young ladies and gentlemen. A nice time, yes. A blast, definitely no."

"Right," Marshall said, but he didn't mean it.

Overnight in a motel. Fifteen kids and just three adult types. The minivan was quiet. We were thinking.

"I can hear your tiny little minds grinding," Molly said. "Don't bother. It's not worth being grounded for the rest of your life. The Hot Shots were eagles. You are chickens."

"Speak for yourself," R.X. said.

The Hot Shots had come home with more

than the trophy. They came back with bags under their eyes. They told stories about staying up until three in the morning eating the pizza they'd ordered out for. Then they'd roamed the halls in their pajamas, pounding on doors. Every hour on the hour they'd phoned the teams they were going to play the next day to keep them from getting any sleep. *They'd* had a real blast.

"Sure, we could do a lot better than they did," R.X. said, and we all knew what he meant. He meant what my dad called hijinks. He meant stuff that could lose me my bike, soccer, and Saturdays till I was a senior in high school. I had a feeling the last thing I needed was a blast.

"I've decided that the team in my story will have to lose their first game," Molly said. "It will be an action-packed, true-to-life heartbreaker. They'll hang their heads in shame. The story judges will love it."

The red light was going on forever.

"If you want to win the contest," I told her, "you've got to be creative. You've got to do something really different. How about this? You tell the story as if you're the soccer ball. You get kicked around—*Bam! Pow!* You split a seam. You almost drown in the mud. You split *two* seams and then you bleed rivers of yellow and red soccer juices all over the field and . . ."

Molly groaned.

The car behind us honked again, long and loud.

"Okay, okay," I said. "That might get rated X for violence. How about this? How about writing it from the point of view of a kid's foot? Teachers love stuff like that. Judges would, too. Every time this kid Molly makes a goal, you could get some great conversations going between the piggy who went to market and the piggy who stayed home."

"It is possible," Molly said, "that you are the most disgusting person I have ever known."

"I feel sick," Lisa said.

"You're not being serious," Molly went on. "I'm going to make this the most exciting story ever. This is a big-time contest. When I win I get to go to Washington, D.C."

Nick turned around and grinned at her. "Forever?" he asked, like he could hardly wait.

She banged him on the head with her notebook.

The little red car passed us. The guy inside it was still leaning on the horn. Lisa pressed her face against the window and stuck her tongue out at him.

"I need to go *bad,*" Toby said.

"I need quiet," Mrs. Rossi said, "bad." She wheeled around the corner, gunned the motor, and we sprayed through the flooded side street like a motor boat.

3. Where Is There?

"Real life," Nick said, "is better than any story Molly Bosco could write." He lowered his voice. "Especially the real life *we're* going to have at the Megadome." He turned to me and grinned.

I hadn't told anybody about my real-life problems with my dad, the police, and the guy from Satinsheen Cement. If I did, that's all they'd talk about. Nick would call me Cement-sicker. He does sometimes anyway because he knows that's what I called cement mixers when I was little. Cement-sickers. I think he likes the way it sounds. If *he* called me that, then everybody would.

"I'll read you what I've got so far," Molly said. "You'll see."

Mrs. Rossi made waves down the street.

Lisa popped the window open again.

R.X. moaned. "Save me."

Molly poked him in the ribs, took a deep breath and began. " 'The rain was falling sideways.' " She stopped and looked around like she thought we should clap. When we didn't, she went on. " 'Big black velvety clouds hung low over the murky motel by the side of the long, winding road. Wild shrieks screamed down its dank, dark halls.' "

"Shrieks don't scream," Lisa told her. "You'll have to change that. It sounds weird."

"It's not weird, it's creative," Molly explained. " 'Wild shrieks screamed down its dank, dark halls,' " she read again, like that was the way it was going to *be.* " 'The stench was like sour milk.' Don't you love that word 'stench'? Can't you just *smell* it?" She didn't wait for an answer. " 'And that was the very place where the Daring Devastators soccer team would spend the long, sickening night.' "

Mrs. Rossi dropped anchor at a light.

"Wait a minute. Have you stayed at this motel?" Marshall asked her, "or is this stuff just out of your head?"

"The real thing cannot be as strange and mysterious as what is in my head," Molly told him. "No way."

"I hear they've got a pool," R.X. said. "I brought my suit."

"And a sauna," Lisa said. "I hear you don't wear anything in saunas. Or maybe that's just—"

Molly cut in. " '*Little* did the Daring Devastators know it would be a night they would always remember. Little did they guess it would be a night they would always regret.' How's that for an opener? Good, or what? I hate first drafts, though. You never know what happens next."

I didn't like it, especially the "always regret" part.

"I don't like it," Toby said. "It sounds like a haunted house."

"In my story it will be *slightly* haunted," Molly said.

"Do I have to sleep in a haunted house?" Toby asked in a voice that would scare away any ghost.

"Right," Nick said. "Turn right at the next stop light and, if I'm not holding this map upside down, the motel should be about a block away."

"Got it," his mom called back.

I looked down at my watch. "Listen," I whispered to Nick, "I don't want to panic anybody, but it's nineteen minutes to game time."

"Molly," Marshall said, "our soccer team is not now and never will be the Daring Devastators. We voted that name down, you may remember, thirteen to one."

"It's a perfect team name," Molly said. "It's miles better than Zappers. That's stupid. Anyway, it's my story. I can use any name I want to. Daring Devastators goes perfectly with the names of the kids in my story. They're Dumdum, Dracula, Desiree, Angel, Killer, and Hulk."

"You're kidding," R.X. said. He checked out her notebook. "She's not kidding," he told us. "Which am I, Killer or Hulk?"

"See, I told you this was amazing," she said.

"When do you get to the good stuff," I asked her, "the talking toes and oozing soccer ball?"

"I bet our real stuff will be better than your fiction stuff," Nick told her.

"Ha!" Molly said. "Fat chance!"

"I bet," Marshall called, "we're almost there. Look, Mrs. Rossi. On the left at the next corner. See the flashing sign? 'Megadome Motel.' And right under it, 'Welcome Players.' That's us."

Mrs. Rossi wheeled into the big circular driveway and pulled up at the entrance.

"Hobie," she said, "run in quick, will you, and find out where your game's supposed to be. Somebody inside must have directions."

I slid the door open and jumped down.

"I've got to *go,*" Toby wailed.

"If you promise to hold it, I'll take you," Nick told him.

"I don't feel so good. Be right back, maybe." Lisa clamped her hand over her mouth and piled out after Nick.

I was the first one through the doors into the motel. For sure this was the right place. The lobby sounded like a gym at game time. Kids in soccer uniforms were hanging out in big clumps, some of them draped over sofas, some of them lying on the floor. A couple dozen bushel baskets of fake vines swung from the ceiling.

"Their goalie," one guy was saying, "heard this girl on the sidelines go, 'He's so *cute.*' Then when he turned his head to smile at her the ball slid right through his legs and into the net."

"And what makes it really funny," a girl went on, "was that she didn't even mean *him.*"

The kids looked a lot as though they'd been wrestling in mud, like if they stopped moving for just two minutes they'd turn into clay statues.

The few adult types were just standing around talking to each other. Nobody seemed to be in charge. Nobody was holding a chart.

Molly's story was right about two things. The air was filled with shrieks and smells. It smelled so much like the chlorine they add to swimming pools, my eyes were watering.

Lisa dashed off down a hall, both hands over her mouth.

"I'll take Toby to the john and then meet you back here," Nick said, and he and Toby followed the arrow with a picture of a man on it.

In front of a counter that said Check In, a long line of people was waiting. Check In sounded right, but hanging around it would have taken an hour. So I ran down a long hall filled with teams of soccer kids, past a candy-bar machine that was calling my name and a game room that was begging for my quarters. Next to the game room was another room filled with people. This one had a sign outside that said Registration.

At last.

Inside, a woman sitting behind a long table was making checks on a clipboard. Next to her a three-foot-tall gold trophy gleamed.

I rushed in. "Could you look on the schedule, please," I asked, "and tell me where the Zappers are supposed to be. I'm in a big hurry. We're late."

She gave me this blank look.

"I'm one of the Zappers," I said, practically gasping for breath. She stared at me like I was maybe a talking frog. "And if we're late, that's it, you know?" I reached over and gave the trophy a pat for luck.

"Can I help you out, young man?" It was an old guy, small and thin, wearing a funny plaid hat with a bill in front *and* in back, like the one Sherlock Holmes wore. "You remind me of one of my grandsons when he's in a hurry," he said. "Slow down, it's going to be all right." The guy didn't look like a coach.

"Where are we supposed to be?" I asked him. He smiled and nodded, but somehow I wasn't sure he understood. "I'm a Zapper," I said a little louder. Everybody in the room turned and stared at me. None of them were kids. "We can't kill these guys unless we're there."

The woman at the table laughed. "I don't know what you're talking about. This is a meeting of W.O.R.M."

I blinked. W.O.R.M. didn't have an *S* in it for soccer.

"World Organization of Readers of Mysteries, is what it is," the guy in the hat said. "Actually, we just had the luncheon kickoff for Who Dun It. That's what this solve-it-yourself murder mystery weekend is called. Excellent meal. The motel has a first-rate chef."

Was this guy crazy? I began to back away.

He stopped smiling. "Do you know about the murder?" he asked. "It could happen any minute, you know."

I knew this was one place I didn't want to be, and so I dashed for the door.

" 'Zapper,' did you say?" he called after me. "And who are you so eager to kill? Do wait, young man. You're not one of our wild-card clues are you?"

Weird. Running back the way I came, I saw

Hello
O. P.
rg ation Rea

that on the other side of the hall from the game room, behind a row of fake palm trees, was the swimming pool. Nobody was in it. It looked good. I'll jump in that water like a cannonball, I decided, right after the game. If there is a game. Which I doubt. I kept moving, dodging kids soaked in rain and muck.

"Those Gazelles are gross," I heard one boy tell another. "They tripped us when the ref wasn't looking, and the tall one stuck her elbow in my ribs twice."

"Do you know who's in charge here?" I asked him.

"Got me," he said, and kept on talking about the gross Gazelles.

Back in the lobby, I watched a soccer ball lob high into the air and land in the middle of one of the vine-filled ceiling baskets. I couldn't tell where it came from, so I didn't know if it was a one-point kick or a two-point hoop.

A girl behind me said, "They're awesome," just like Lisa would say it. I turned to ask her if she'd learned anything, only it wasn't Lisa.

All I'd done was waste time and lose Lisa. And Nick. He wasn't anywhere in sight.

"Young man," a voice behind me yelled. "Zapper, please . . ."

It was the man in the detective hat, so I ducked my head down low and ran. I ran back to the minivan as fast as I could to tell the kids I was sorry.

The rain had stopped. There was almost sun, but that didn't help much.

"Where have you *been*?" Molly asked when I got there. "We've been waiting forever. If we're late it's your fault."

Toby was already strapped back into his kid seat.

"Mom refused to honk the horn for you," Nick said.

"Do you know where we're going?" I asked, pulling the door shut.

"I, like, threw up really fast," Lisa told me. "And then I hurried back because I didn't want to be late. And then of course I had to wait for you. Now I'm starting to feel sick all over again."

"Gun it," R.X. called out, so I guess they knew where they were going.

At two-o-two exactly by my Mickey Mouse

watch, we were sitting in the white minivan at a red light.

"The game is at Veteran's Park," Molly explained to me. "I found the directions." She waved a green sheet of paper in front of my nose. "They were written on the other side of Nick's page, the one that told us how to get to the motel. As soon as I found them, I ran in and saw Nick and Toby right away. Nick was just standing around talking to these girls. The Gazelles."

"I was asking them questions," he told her. "And it wasn't just girls, there were guys, too. It's a mixed team, like us."

"Mixed *up,*" R.X. said.

Molly smiled. "Actually, according to the map, we passed Veteran's Park on our way here."

"Oh, well," Marshall told her, "it's not whether you win or lose, it's whether you make it to the game."

"In my story, they've already lost, big," Molly said. "Poor Daring Devastators." She put the cap on her pen and stuck it in her pocket.

"Gun it," R.X. called.

Mrs. Rossi sighed. And then she gunned it.

If we get there in time, I thought, I'll make

three goals. Or seven. I'll make seven goals, and my dad will say that's amazing and how can you not trust a kid who makes seven goals? The Park District will hire me for lots of money to give advice to all of the coaches. Then I can pay the cement man myself. Happily ever after.

R.X. leaned over and whispered in my ear. "A blast," he said. "We're going to have a blast."

4. It Was the Mud

We drove up honking.

"I don't believe it!" Mr. Star called to us. "You're here! Nine minutes past two, and you're here." He practically hugged us as we piled out of the minivan. "They gave us ten extra minutes because of the storm, and here you are with sixty seconds to spare. In the last twenty minutes I've eaten a whole bag of Tootsie Rolls. If I were a nail biter, my fingers would be stumps."

Across the field the other team was all suited up in matching purple-and-gold warm-up suits. They were standing in a straight line, holding matching purple-and-gold equipment bags, ready to march away with the victory. I waved at them. They looked mad at us for coming, except for one kid, who grinned a mean grin and another who smiled like she wanted to play.

"Let me explain," Mrs. Rossi said, but Mr. Star just shook his head.

"You made it," he told her. "That's all that matters. The rest of the kids are warmed up. And while I really hate to play anybody who's been riding in a car for three or four hours, I'm afraid we've got to this time."

"Hobie and I have been running," Nick explained, like we'd been pacing the car all the way.

"I, personally, am not dying to play right now," Molly told him. "The field looks yucky. And Lisa *can't* go on. She just threw up her bologna sandwich and banana. Did you have cookies, too, Lisa?" Then she whispered to me, "In my story she'll be sick because of the rattlesnake sandwich her mother packed by mistake, and she'll spend three days in the dank, dark motel bed."

Mr. Star looked us over. "Okay, we'll start Nick and Hobie—though I don't believe for a second you've been exercising. And R.X., you'll have to finish suiting up, too. All of you stretch, at least, and let's huddle."

We stuck shin guards under our socks, pulled up on one ankle until we kicked ourselves, did the same stretch with the other leg, and that was that for warm-ups.

"Took you long enough to get here," Aretha said.

R.X. shrugged. He didn't tell her it was his fault. "Slow's okay," he said. "The tortoise beat the hare."

"Sure. But he had to show up on time to do it," Aretha said.

Just as our whole team gathered in a circle the sun went behind the clouds, like it had made a mistake and this was one game it really didn't want to watch. The rain began to fall again, too—big, fat blobs of it.

"Now I want you all to get out there and hustle," Mr. Star told us. "The other team are the Pigs, the Pittsfield Pigs. We've been watching them practice, and they look as though they're pretty good. But then, you'd almost have to be good if you're going to be called Pigs."

"I thought they were the Pits," Lisa said. "Somebody told me that."

"No, I hear they're a fine team," Mr. Star explained. "But then so are you. It's going to be slippery out there for both sides. All you have to do is remember to hustle, to keep your eye on the ball, think fast, play as a team, mark your players, use the whole field, and have a good time."

"And win," Lisa said.

"That, too, if possible," he told us.

We put our hands together. We yelled, "Go, Zappers!" Then all of us went to the field but Molly and Lisa. They ran to the minivan. Toby, who didn't even belong in the huddle, skipped back to a bench on the sidelines where his mom was sitting covered with a big khaki tarp. Aretha's dad, Mr. Cabell, was walking up and down under a huge orange-and-black umbrella, yelling, "Go, Zappers!"

Even in the rain the Pigs looked good in their purple and gold. We had red letters ironed on our white tee-shirts. Most of the shirts said ZAPPERS. R.X, though, had peeled off three letters, so his said A PE S. Our shorts were white, too. The better to see us with.

First off, we lost the toss. And you could tell just by the way the Pigs moved that they knew what they were doing. They looked like they'd been dribbling balls while we were still drooling on bibs.

The mud sucked at my soles every step I took. The Pigs passed the ball down the field toward our goal using really solid footwork. They were keeping their eyes on the ball, they were hustling, they were yelling things to each other like, "Nice ball," "Trailer," "Cross it." The mud did not, for some reason, seem to suck at their feet.

Their goalie was huge. She must have been a sixth grader. She stood like a giant gorilla at the end of the field with her knees bent, her arms out, and a killer look in her eyes. You could see it, even through the rain. She was wearing an orange-and-silver shirt, industrial strength gloves, enormous knee pads, and a vest that looked bulletproof.

Our goalie was Trevor. His red, white, and blue sweat shirt had green iron-on letters. Mr. Star keeps telling us you are what you eat. Trevor eats marshmallow and chocolate sandwiches for lunch. On white bread. He was doing almost everything right, though. His feet were pointing outward, shoulder-width apart. His knees and back were bent just enough. His elbows were

se to his body like Mr. Star had told
hands were in front of his face. He
my. He didn't want to go home
d.

pass," Nick yelled. I saw a small
cking the ball across me toward
a re it was, flying free with my
na

I s, hauled back, stiffened my
ankle forward, and kicked. But
when high enough, there was
nothing ir, wet air. It was a total
whiff. I seam of the ball.

By the t yself from a mud hole,
the action else. This was not a
good start o So far there wasn't
anything to m d he'd let me come.

"Suuuuuuuu- Pigs were yelling.
The ones on the ones on the bench,
all of them were pu ping their arms and screaming hog-calling cheers.

Somehow the ball had slipped past Trevor and
into the net.

It had taken maybe three minutes for the score
to be Pigs 1, Zappers 0.

"Quack, quack, quack," I heard from somewhere. It was Toby, sitting on his mother's lap, his head sticking out of the tarp. He was cheering us on.

"Heads up, Zappers," Mr. Cabell yelled. He had given up his umbrella for a camcorder. Tape does not lie. I stuck out my tongue as the camera zoomed in.

The rain stopped. The sun had changed its mind and was looking down at us. Lisa and Molly climbed out of the minivan.

Lisa began her cheerleading routine. It was, I think, a cheer she had written herself.

"Underneath the soccer field,
Worms and ants.
Think you can beat us?
You'll lose your pants.
Yaaaaaaaaaaay, team!"

She jumped high and bounced up and down on her toes.

"Don't blow it," Molly called to us.

None of us *wanted* to blow it, so when we got the ball back at center field we started moving it toward their goal. The ball skipped past me, somehow, and I gave a power kick, instead, to this guy's ankle. He yelped, curled his lip, and called me a cheater, but I didn't mean to do it, no kidding. This was the guy with the mean grin.

A very small Pig captured the ball I meant to get, and started dribbling it toward Trevor.

"Mark your players," Mr. Star called to us from the sidelines.

"*Do* something!" Molly yelled, and Aretha did. She caught the ball with her shoulder, knocked it to Marshall, and we were on a roll again.

We were on a roll for about thirty seconds. The ball sloshed back and forth in the middle of the field. The Pigs in their fancy uniforms weren't doing any better than we were. They kept yelling, "Square," changing positions, and passing the ball sideways, only to have it get sopped up in a puddle. It was the field against everybody.

The whole first half we slogged along without another point for either team. Their ball hit the side of our net twice. Our ball came within half an inch of rocketing in once. It would have, too, but the giant somehow got her paw on it.

At the second half Molly and Lisa came in. That didn't help, either. Molly blasted a line drive into the bushes. Then, ten minutes into the second half, Hobie Hanson, hero, got the ball in the clear and oozed it down the field.

Our whole group on the sidelines was yelling, "Go, Zappers," except, of course, Toby, who was quacking.

Suddenly, I saw Nick right there in front of me in goal-scoring position. I passed the ball toward him and watched it skip across the grass in slow motion.

"Shoot!" Molly yelled.

Nick took a deep breath and shot. He didn't kick with the side of his foot, though, like you're supposed to. He toe-jammed it. Aiming with his big toe, he kicked straight on. His aim was true, so that might even have worked, but the mud sucking at his shoe had ripped his sole wide open.

That's why, when he kicked, his foot stuck for a second in the ooze. In that second the ball flew past. That didn't stop Nick. He kept kicking. As he raised his leg, his shoe scooped a gob of mud out of the field and into the air. Nick had a terrific follow-through.

The goalie saw the black mush coming straight at her. She held out her hand, but the stuff spread as it flew. Only half of it landed in her glove. The other half slapped her flat in the face. And I think that may be why she didn't keep her eye on the ball.

Nick had missed the ball, but Aretha hadn't. Aretha caught it with her arch and flipped it, zap, into the net, right past the gooey goalie.

Pigs 1, Zappers 1.

"Foul," the Pigs' coach yelled.

"Quackquackquackquack," Toby screamed. He was jumping up and down in a puddle.

"Ugh, ugh, ugh, ugh," the Pigs grunted. One or two of them looked as though they were thinking about illegal use of their hands.

There was a major argument about whether mud in the eye is a foul if it's kicked there by total mistake. Mr. Star said no way. The Pigs' coach shook his fist at Mr. Star and said it was a dirty trick. The referee ended up saying that while it was for sure dirty, he wasn't going to call it foul.

All we'd really done, though, was to make them mad, and we found out right away that you don't want to mess around with a wet fieldful of mad Pigs.

The kids on their sidelines—and there were a lot of them—started in with hog grunts again instead of suuuuuueeeees. Then they chanted "ugh, ugh, ugh, ugh, ugh." And while it didn't sound as good as Lisa's cheer, it seemed to work a whole lot better. The rest of the game they pretty much owned the ball.

Purple and gold swam down the field. They kicked.

Trevor stuck out both arms. The ball spun through his legs.

"Suuuuuuueeeeeeeee! Ugh!"

And again.

"Suuuuuuuueeeeeeeeee! Ugh! Ugh!"

And one more time.

"Suuuuuuuuuueeeeeeeeeeee! Ugh! Ugh! Ugh!"

The final score was Pigs 4, Zappers 1.

While we sloshed off the field, the Pigs marched in a straight line to their school bus, with their coach going, "You're winners. Look like it. Shoulders back. Hut, two, three, four."

It could have been worse. We still had our health. And, as Mr. Star pointed out, there was always tomorrow.

5. You Did It!

"Okay, so tomorrow's another game," Nick said, as we hauled our bags into the motel. "But just take a look at this place. From now *till* tomorrow is going to be such a blast."

"Don't be silly," Molly told him. "This is just a motel. It's not even dank and haunted like the one in my story. I've decided that, except for the girl who's poisoned with rancid rattlesnake meat and the kid who turns into a werewolf, my Daring Devastators will watch some TV, eat a healthy supper, and then get a good night's rest. That's what motels are for. To rest."

"You're going to win a prize with rest?" I asked her.

"Actually, while their eyes are closed, I'm going to have a fairy godmother cast a spell on their soccer ball so the next day they win ninety-four to nothing. You've got to have a happy ending."

Marshall shrugged. "So, now what'll *we* do?" he asked Nick. "You got any happy endings in mind for us?"

"I expect," Molly told him, "that you should keep moving or your pants will turn into clay pots. Then you would *not* have a happy ending." She tucked her notebook under her arm, picked up her suitcase, and hurried off to join a clump of girls.

"Moving sounds good to me," I said. "Maybe we could start with a swim. In that big stand of fake palm trees over there is a real live pool of water." We couldn't get into any trouble swimming in the pool. That's what it's there for.

"You kids stay close by, now," Mr. Star said. "I'm going to check us in."

The check-in line was still backed up, with eight or ten coaches standing in front of Mr. Star. Figuring it was going to take him half an hour at least, we all fanned out to look the place over.

R.X. had already wandered off, so Nick and Marshall and I checked out the small, dark game room. It was wall-to-wall kids. You could hear the thwack, thwack, thwack of helicopters, the blops of exploding asteroids, the skids of cars screeching around mountain curves, and, on top of that, the clang of the change machine dropping token after token after token. The noise made your eyes shake in their sockets.

"Excellent," Marshall said, "but we'd have to stand in line practically forever. Besides, it costs a lot of quarters, which we don't have." This was true. I sure didn't. We watched for a while. A kid who said he'd just won his soccer game ten–zip racked up a zillion points and the machine played him a victory song that went on practically forever. We left before it was over.

Dragging our duffels behind us, we headed into this humongous four-story atrium with a dome over it. All around us, when we looked up, we could see rows and rows and rows of motel rooms with fancy white-iron balconies.

Down near where we stood there was a Camelot miniature golf course with castles and dragons and windmills. Little plastic knights sat on horses, and small ladies with cones on their heads leaned out of towers. That was on one side of the atrium. On the other side was the swimming pool.

"Where you think you're going?" a man asked us.

We were going to see how warm the water was, is all. We weren't going to jump in with our muddy clothes on or anything.

"Pool area's off limits today," he told us. "We're workin' here." He and a lot of other people were setting up chairs and tables.

"No swimming? Bummer!" Marshall groaned.

"I bet they're getting ready for tomorrow's awards ceremony," Nick said. "That's probably where they're going to give out trophies to all the teams who didn't fall flat on their faces in the mud."

"Look at that!" Marshall grabbed my arm and pointed up. "Watch him," he said. "He'll never make it." A kid in a muddy soccer shirt was leaning over one of the top-floor balconies. He was aiming a blue ball at another kid standing on a balcony all the way across the atrium. To make it, the kid would need the arm of a White Sox pitcher.

He cranked it up and let it fly. The ball started to sink almost as soon as it left the kid's hand. It missed the palm trees. But we watched as it curved down toward the fifth hole of the golf course. It was falling toward a man who was aiming his putter. What he was trying to do was hit the ball through the pink castle before its drawbridge went up. The bridge went up about every thirty seconds. Maybe the guy was always a klutz with a putter and would have landed his golf ball in the water anyway. But it really put him off his shot, you could tell, when the blue ball from the balcony slapped him on the top of his head.

Actually, what landed on his head wasn't a ball. It didn't bounce. It popped. What it was, really, was a fat, sloppy water balloon that went kaplooie the second it hit.

The golfer yelped. Loud. It was easy to see why, too, because his nose and both his ears were dripping and a gush of water was draining down his back. He dropped the golf club, grabbed his neck, and started shaking his fist, but he didn't know where to shake it. Two or three people pointed up, but by then both kids had disappeared. The soggy man didn't have a clue where the water balloon had come from.

"Now that's something we could do tonight instead of sleep," Nick said. "We could toss water grenades."

"Young man, don't move," somebody yelled, and we all three turned around. On the fake grass rug behind us we'd tracked in big blobs of soccer mud. We looked at the mess. We looked at each other. It was pretty clear that if we ran we'd keep leaving a trail that was easier to follow than Hansel and Gretel's.

"Zapper!" the same voice called and a small

old man came puffing up to us. It was the guy with the detective hat I'd run into before the game. "I can't run as fast as I used to," he said, fanning himself with his notebook.

"Listen, we didn't mean to do it," Nick told him, kicking a clod of mud toward a palm tree.

"You *did* it?" the man asked, practically shouting, his face getting as red as his bow tie. "I can't believe you're telling me. I never thought I'd be the one to solve the mystery. Never. Here we've got until midnight to solve the crime and I already know who did it." He lowered his voice. "You haven't told anybody else, have you?"

We stared at him. I wasn't sure what to say. Marshall and Nick looked at each other and rolled their eyes. You could tell they thought he was a few spokes short of a wheel. "Haven't told a soul," Nick said, and he laughed.

"You must be older than you look," the old man went on. "With all the mud it's hard to tell. Even wearing your disguise, though," he told me, "I was sure the minute I saw you that you were a clue." Then, glancing around to see if anybody was watching, he lowered his voice even more. "I don't think you were supposed to admit it right away, but I do thank you."

"You're welcome," Nick said, and he and Marshall both laughed, which was pretty mean.

The old man smiled at them. "Now all I must do," he said, "is find out exactly *how* you did it." He pulled out a small gold pen and opened his notebook.

"Wait a minute," I told him. "Slow down. You've made a big mistake." I didn't want this nice old guy to think we were the answer to his mystery. "All we're guilty of is tracking in a little dirt. We've got muddy feet, but we don't have bloody hands. We don't know anything about your murder."

The old man chuckled like I'd told a good joke. "Teasing won't work," he said. "You've already confessed."

"Murder?" Nick grabbed me by the arm. "What murder?"

"Bloody hands?" Marshall asked, holding his out. He had a Big Bird bandage wrapped around his right thumb.

People were stopping to stare.

"The W.O.R.M. folks said a first timer didn't have a chance." The guy grinned. "Did I tell you my children and grandchildren gave me this weekend for my seventieth birthday? The grandchildren are the ones who thought of it. They are going to be so proud. Tell me, did you kill him with poison chocolate cake? That's my theory. You know, because of the crumbs on his mouth and hands. And why did he die next to the ice-making machine? Was he trying to tell us something?"

The man wasn't listening to us. He was believing what he wanted to believe.

"We didn't *do* it," I told him. Somehow I sounded guilty. Maybe it was the trail of mud.

"Hobie, Nick, Marshall! Come to the elevators right now." The voice sounded like it was blasting through a bullhorn. It was Molly. "Mr. Star is ready to kill you!"

"Kill you? Oh, they wouldn't do that, would they? You're such nice young men," the nice old man said, shaking his head. "I understand that you can't tell me everything. They do provide us with clues, of course, but people are saying that some of the clues are missing. Please, if there are any details you can give me, call anytime." He wrote something on a piece of paper and handed it to me.

"Ho-beeeeee," Molly yelled, and we all three dashed toward the lobby.

"That guy would be perfect for Molly's story," Marshall said as we ran. "He's about as mysterious as you get."

"Did the missing necklace have anything to do with it?" the man called after us.

"Nothing at all," Nick called back, laughing. "What a weirdo."

"What was *that* about?" Marshall asked, as we cruised toward Molly and the bank of elevators.

While we ran I told them as much as I knew, which wasn't much. The guy would find out, I figured, in maybe five minutes that we hadn't pretended to poison a perfectly innocent chocolate cake. I stuck the paper he'd given me in my pocket, though. I didn't want to be found guilty of mud-tracking *and* littering.

"Took you long enough," Molly said when we got there, but we weren't even the last ones to show. None of the adult types was there, and half the team was missing.

"Where'd you guys go?" R.X. asked. "I looked all over. You left me here with the girls. You're always ditching me."

We didn't mean to ditch R.X. It just happened. I shrugged.

He made a face back. "Mr. Star is still dragging

kids out of the game room," he went on. "He told me that as soon as all three of you guys got here we could go on up." R.X. grabbed his bag from a big pile of them and pressed the elevator button. Then he waggled the key in his hand so we could see it. "Third-floor room," he said. "It's ours for the night."

"Our own room? You've got to be kidding." Nick shook his head. "They'd put the four of us together?"

Marshall laughed. "This is amazing. This will, in fact, be the most excellent overnight ever."

"Think of the crazy stuff we can do," I said, and then I remembered that the last thing I needed was crazy stuff.

"Right," Molly said. "What you'll really do is get ten quiet hours of sleep. The girls, on the other hand . . ." She smiled.

The elevator doors opened. "Forget Molly," R.X. called. "Listen to *me.*" As he stepped in, a bunch of people pushed out around us. R.X. kept talking. "Mr. Star told me . . ."

We grabbed our duffels to go with him, but before we could make it inside, the elevator doors slapped shut. We stood there holding the bags.

6. Pig Out in the Hall

When the next elevator came, the three of us got inside.

"Before you do anything else," Molly called, "take off those dirty clothes and put them in a pile. Mr. Star says he's going to find some way to wash them before tomorrow's game."

The doors shut.

"You guys do look a lot like mudmen," Nick said. "But *my* stuff's not so bad. Except maybe the socks. I think they used to move when I wiggled my toes."

"Push three," Marshall told him. "R.X. said we're on the third floor."

Nick pushed three. "We have to remember to call Molly in the middle of the night to prove we're awake," he said.

The elevator stopped at the second floor. The doors opened and a kid in a blue-and-green soccer uniform dashed in. He crouched on the floor behind us. "Don't let on I'm here," he whispered. "I don't want them to see me."

Outside the elevator nobody was looking in, but we scrunched together like a wall in front of him, anyway. When the doors shut, I looked back at the kid.

"Who are you hiding from?" I asked him. "Does the old guy in the detective hat think you did it, too?"

"Did what?" he asked.

"The murder," Nick told him.

The kid stood up fast, his back to the wall. "What murder?" His eyes searched the ceiling, as if maybe there was an emergency exit up the elevator cables and through the roof.

"Victim was found dead on the third floor somewhere around two o'clock," Marshall explained. "They're looking for suspicious characters. Know anything about it?"

"I don't know about any murder," the kid said. "No kidding. I'm just playing elevator tag. The only one who's after me is Cadenza. That's the girl who's It."

Just as the elevator stopped on three, the kid began to edge around us. Before the doors had opened all the way, he escaped. A girl in a blue-and-green shirt was waiting for him.

"Cadenza!" He practically hugged her.

"Caught you, Roscoe," she said, but she hadn't. He'd run straight to her, away from us.

"I *knew* you'd get off on three," she told him. "You're so predictable. *I* ran up the stairs." They both took off down the hall.

"Elevator tag." Nick pulled his duffle into the hall. "That's another thing we could do. We could play elevator tag at midnight. If we do," he said, whomping Marshall on the back, "you're It."

"Hurry up, you guys," R.X. called from around the corner. "I'm always losing you. I found our room." We dragged down the hall to the doorway where he was standing with his blue bag.

"Except, for some reason, the stupid key doesn't work," he said.

"Try turning it the other way up," Marshall told him.

"I already tried. It's totally broken. Wouldn't you know."

"Let me." I grabbed the key, but before I even had a chance to jab it in, the door swung wide open.

For sure this wasn't our room, but I knew the kid who was standing there. And he knew me. He was a Pig. He was the sneering Pig whose toes I'd crunched in the mud.

"Hey, you guys," he called into the room, "guess who's trying to huff and puff and blow our door down. It's four of the Zippers. Remember the late, not-so-great Slipper Zippers, the team that came apart at the shoe seams?" His lip curled way up on one side like he smelled skunk.

A big gang of Pigs gathered at the door behind him. They were still dressed in purple, gold, and dirt. "The Zippers," they said all together.

"That's the one who gave Magdalena a mouthful of mud." The smallest boy pointed at Nick.

"She's still mad, you know. I wouldn't want Magdalena mad at me. She gave Quint here a bloody nose once, didn't she, Quint?"

The kid with the sneer did not answer the boy's question. He asked his own. "You're the cheater who stepped on my foot, aren't you?" He pointed at my nose.

R.X. grabbed the key from my hand and ran.

"Sorry," I told them. "Wrong room."

"You want to come in?" the little kid asked. "It's safe. Magdalena's not here, and Quint wouldn't normally hurt a flea."

"We've got big plans for tonight," the Quint kid said. "Our coach doesn't care what we do. We'll probably go to the club next door. They've got a band." The Pigs moved toward us. "We're going to have us a time," Quint said. "Tonight is going to be wild and crazy."

We backed away and headed down the hall to where R.X. was trying to open the next door.

The Pigs watched. There were a lot more of them than there were of us.

That lock wasn't working either. "It's a bad key," R.X. explained.

When the door finally opened it wasn't the

key that did it. It was Lisa, who opened it a crack, just as far as the chain would reach—about two inches. "The boys are here!" she called. The girls inside shrieked. "What do you want?" she asked us.

The hall was beginning to fill with Pigs. They looked dangerous. They looked like they were about to grunt. They looked like guys to get away from.

"Zip-pers," they chanted, "Zip-pers."

"Let us in," R.X. demanded.

"Don't be silly." Lisa slammed the door.

"What do we do now?" R.X. was about to fling the key down the hall, when Lisa opened the door again. She stuck out her arm and fastened a sign around the doorknob. Do Not Disturb, it said.

Marshall grabbed the key from R.X. "Maybe," he said, "there's some kind of clue on this thing, like a number." He held it up to the light. "What do you know, it says 306, *not* this room or the last room. Let's try the next door down."

"It's not my fault," R.X. said, moving on. "The hall doesn't have enough light in it."

One of the Pigs bounced a soccer ball on the ceiling behind us.

Marshall stabbed the key into the lock of the room numbered 306, turned it, and pushed. The door opened. Nobody jumped out and called us names. Nobody screamed. Nobody met us at all as we rushed in and slammed the door.

We stood there in the dark. *Plunk,* we heard, *plunk,* as the soccer ball hit the walls outside.

"Hey, you. Hey, you slippery Zippers," the Quint kid called, "we're going to practice a little ball out here. How about a rematch?"

7. Bummer!

We flipped on a light. The first thing I saw was the TV. It was a big one, with a cable box on top. Terrific! Never can tell what you might see on cable. We could switch channels until four in the morning and nobody would know. And if nobody knew, nobody could tell my dad. I was home free.

There were two big beds with a telephone in between them. All night long we could call the girls' room and then hang up. Next to the wall was a rollaway cot waiting to be opened. And at the end of the room were these full-length glass doors that slid open to let you walk onto a balcony. We'd lucked into a room that looked out over the Megadome atrium and down onto the swimming pool and the miniature golf course and palm trees and all those people who wouldn't have a clue where a water balloon came from when it hit them on the head. It was the best room. And it was ours, all ours.

"Looks like somebody's got to sleep on the floor," Nick said. "There are three beds and four of us."

"I call I get a big bed," Marshall called.

"Me, too," I said.

"No fair," Nick complained. "Okay, I'll take the cot since I don't plan to sleep much anyway. Looks like a very soft rug, R.X. You're going to love it."

"I've got news for you guys. All four of us will be sleeping in the big beds." R.X. said, flopping down on one of them. "I was going to tell you, only you kept talking to Molly and then the elevator door shut in my face. See, before he gave me the key, Mr. Star said he was putting all the main troublemakers in the same room so he could keep an eye on us."

"What's that supposed to mean?" Marshall asked.

"That means," R.X. said, grabbing the remote control, "that we're doubling up on the double beds. The cot is for Mr. Star."

That couldn't be true. That would ruin everything. "Mr. Star will be *here*?" I asked. "In this room? With us? All night?"

R.X. nodded. "Here. In this room. With the main troublemakers."

"Bummer," we said, almost together.

"Molly's right," Nick said. "We'll get ten hours' sleep. He'll have us showered, shampooed, teeth brushed, fingernails cleaned, and tucked in by nine o'clock. He'll unplug the TV, review today's game, and tell us a bedtime story."

Boring, I thought. But if my dad heard that line-up, he'd probably buy me a *new* bicycle.

"Bummer," Marshall said again.

R.X. clicked on the TV.

Thump, we heard from the hall, *thump.* Those lucky Pigs were still thwacking the ball against the walls and ceiling. They would be up all night eating triple-cheese pizza, playing Marco Polo in the pool, feeding the game machines, sneaking out to hear the band next door, and then having a really, really wild and crazy time bugging us.

I peeled off my dirt shirt. Nick kicked off his mud-clogged shoes.

"My mom says she can get these fixed," he said. "But I think they are dead. Tomorrow I'll have to wear my sneakers." He threw himself on the bed.

Thump! Thump! We all four sat there listening to the Pigs hit the hall ceiling with their ball, and watching the Weather Channel man talk about highs *Thump!* and lows *Thump!* and slow-moving storm systems. *Thump! Thump!*

"Boys!" A deep voice echoed down the hall.

Was it Mr. Star, checking up on us already? R.X. flipped off the TV.

"Boys!" The voice was closer. "What is the meaning of this behavior?" It was not Mr. Star, but we held our breaths, listening. "Certainly not what I expected," it went on. "Can't I leave you gentlemen alone for ten minutes? Quint, could that possibly be you? I am amazed, astonished, dismayed. All right, I want you to line up, right where you are, and march directly back to the room. Hut, two, three, four."

" 'March?' This I've got to see." I hurried to the door, flung it open and stuck my head out to watch the Pigs march.

Most of them were way at the end of the hall, next to the pop and ice-making machines.

"Move!" their coach barked, and they moved.

We all four stood at the door and grinned as they passed by. None of them grinned back. The little kid was carrying the ball under his arm. We didn't say a thing, but then, we didn't have to. They knew *we* knew they wouldn't be doing any wild and crazy things tonight at all.

Quint was the last one in line. He wasn't marching, though. He was shuffling along slow. He was dribbling a small grayish ball between his

feet, and as he reached our door he kicked it sideways. The kid had an amazing kick. The ball slid through our room all the way to the glass balcony doors, where it hit and bounced away.

"Quint," the deep voice boomed, "did you knock something into that room? What was it?"

"Nothing," Quint said, and he shrugged.

"Boys," the coach asked us, "what did my team member kick into your room?"

We looked at each other and copied Quint's shrug.

"Nothing," Nick said, slamming the door

so the coach couldn't come in and search.

We searched. All four of us had our heads on the floor, peering under beds and chairs searching for it when the phone rang.

"Did you take your clothes off yet?" Molly asked, as soon as I picked it up.

"What?" I asked her. "What are you saying?"

"Your dirty clothes. You've got to have them ready in a neat pile near the door in five minutes because that's when Mr. Star is coming to pick them up. He's going to take them out to a Laundromat. The motel's washer and dryer stopped working. Mr. Cabell just called. He said to tell everybody, and that's what I'm doing.

"Tie your socks together so they'll stay in pairs and not get mixed up with everybody else's. Also, don't leave anything valuable in your pockets. Anything you leave will die in the dryer if it doesn't get killed in the washer first."

"I've put clothes in the laundry before. I'm not stupid," I told her.

"Right," she said. "Also, Mr. Cabell says to keep away from the action in the atrium, that you'd only be in the way. Good-bye."

I hung up.

"They're collecting our dirty clothes in five

minutes," I said to the group. "Nick, look and see what's happening in the atrium. Molly said to stay away from it."

"I'm not putting on clean clothes without taking a shower," R.X. said, and slammed the bathroom door. "That would be disgusting."

I took off my shoes and socks. There was a line where the socks ended. A shower wouldn't have been a bad idea, but R.X. was already in it, singing.

Nick slid open the glass doors and stepped out onto the balcony. Then he hurried back in. "We've got to get down there. What's happening is bizarre. You're not going to believe this."

"So many kids in the pool it's flooding the golf course?" Marshall asked, emptying his duffel on the floor between the beds.

I kicked my dirty clothes into a heap next to the TV and pulled on clean ones. The shirt and jeans looked okay, but my face and arms belonged with the dirty set.

R.X. was still singing in the shower. "Great, green gobs . . ."

Nick started shedding his mud suit. "Hurry up," he told us. "The music's already started. This is going to be amazing."

"What music?" Marshall asked, tying his shoes.

Nick got dressed in thirty seconds flat.

"Shouldn't we wait for R.X.?" I asked him. R.X. was still singing, filling the shower with "Great green gobs of greasy grimy gopher guts . . ."

"He'll find us," Nick said. "Hurry it up. I don't know how long the music will last."

We kicked our dirty clothes into a pile for Mr. Star.

"What music?" Marshall asked again, brushing the dirt out of his hair.

Nick opened the door into the hall. "It's 'Here Comes the Bride,' " he said, "and wait till you see the bride."

8. I Do!

The bride had a red ball on her nose and a red fright wig on her head. Otherwise, from the neck down, she looked pretty normal. I mean, she was wearing a long white dress like brides do in magazines. She wasn't holding anything weirder than a bunch of pink roses.

The groom had on this white tuxedo with a pink flower in the lapel. His nose and hair seemed okay, but his smile was green. It was painted on, over about half his face. His regular mouth was smiling, too.

There must have been sixty or seventy wedding guests, standing around near the pool where we'd seen the guys setting up tables and chairs. They'd even put a little white fence up to keep outsiders from wandering in.

All of the chairs had pink and silver balloons tied to them on long strings so they floated high and bumped against each other. They looked nice.

None of the guests seemed weird. You wouldn't have looked twice if you'd met them walking down the street.

"What did I tell you?" Nick asked. "Was this worth running down the steps for or what?"

Nick and Marshall hurried over to the grove of fake palm trees, where Molly and Lisa were standing with their mouths open. Way on the other side of the pink miniature golf castle I could see the old man from the mystery club. He was still taking notes.

"Isn't this cute beyond belief?" I heard a lady behind me ask. "One of the cutest wedding receptions I ever saw in my whole livelong days. I left my desk in bookkeeping just to watch. If anybody wants their bill right now they can just forget it. I wasn't going to miss a minute of this. I was in on the planning of it, you know." She reached over my shoulder and waved at somebody across the room. "I bet you don't know why the bride and groom are dressed like that, do you?"

The woman with her grunted.

"Well, I just happened to talk to the bride's mother when she reserved the atrium for the party. That's how I know. She told me that the bride and groom met at Klown Kollege in Florida. It's a school where people learn to be funny. They learn to stand on their heads and make strange noises, I guess. Anyway, the two of them fell in love with their funny faces on."

"It's downright silly," the woman with her said. "The things people think of! This marriage will never last."

I didn't see why not. At least they liked the same things. On TV you're always seeing snorkling weddings or skydiving weddings. I didn't remember one with clowns before. Lots of people were taking their pictures; not just the wedding guests, either. For four stories up, the dome was filled with little white flashing stars. In the beginning I'd thought for sure this was part of the old man's mystery game, but it looked like a real, live, weird wedding party.

I backed up closer to the women to find out what I could.

"Of *course* it will work. It's a sweet, sweet story," the lady explained to her friend. "The bride is a local girl. Isn't that lovely? Her parents are paying for it. Look at those heaps of shrimp. Next to them are tiny sausages wrapped in puff pastry. I can tell you that spread cost a bundle. And, my dear, it's only the chef at our Megadome who can make ice sculpture so lifelike."

I craned my neck to look at the sculpture. It was on a table near the swimming pool and it was carved out of blue ice that was taller than I was. The ice thing looked to me like a tall frozen *j*.

"That's lifelike?" said the woman who thought the whole thing was silly. "Well, then, you just tell me what life it's like."

"I can't actually see from here what it is," the lady from bookkeeping answered, sounding annoyed. "It may be her little clown nose and his big clown shoes. I *do* know that they're serving small *Z*'s shaped out of orange Jell-O. That's because they are the new Mr. and Mrs. Zemek. Jell-O *Z*'s, isn't that cute!"

I think I shouldn't have laughed, because the

lady leaned over, grabbed my collar, and said, "Young man, your ears are dirty. And you ought to know better than to use them for eavesdropping."

I said I was sorry even though I wasn't. People started shushing us, so I hurried away to tell Nick and Marshall what I'd learned. All around the atrium people were hanging over their balconies, watching. R.X. was on ours. I waved, but he wasn't looking. He seemed to be talking to a bunch of Pigs, on their balcony two rooms over. I watched as Quint tossed a soccer ball into the air, caught it, and then threw it across the girls' room toward R.X. He put up his hands, but it flew right past him and landed on the balcony floor. I could see the Pigs pointing and laughing.

It didn't look like much fun. R.X. must be waiting for us, I thought. As soon as I told the guys about Klown Kollege I'd wave him down. I made my way toward the clump of Zappers.

"You're not going to believe this," I said when I got there. "I found out why—"

"Shhhhhh," Molly hissed. "He's about to kiss the bride."

That meant it was time to say "yuck." Ordinarily I wouldn't even have *looked* at the dumb kiss,

but this wasn't going to be an ordinary dumb kiss. From there I could see the groom's shoes. They were green and purple and the fronts of them were as big as dinner plates. They were so big they kept him from standing close to her. When he puckered up and leaned way over to reach her, all four stories of that huge space got dead quiet. It was so quiet that when he finally did kiss her the only sound you could hear was her red nose honking.

The bride and groom turned and bowed. On four floors of balconies people were laughing and clapping.

"This is great stuff," I told Molly. "We don't even need to stay up all night. The Hot Shots never did anything as good as this." What's more, I thought, it can't get me into any deep water.

A woman sitting at a big white piano near the pool began to play as the bride and groom moved around hugging people.

"Maybe this is good enough for you," Molly said. "But Lisa and I are going to do more than watch. We're going to meet the bride and groom. We're going to ask them why they're dressed like that. It's research for my story."

"We're *what*?" Lisa yelped, but Molly grabbed her by the elbow and pushed her straight for the balloons.

The place was going crazy. Even over the aahing and oohing and laughing and music, though, you could hear, from three floors up, a voice boom out. "Gentlemen," it said, "it's time to see the game video. Inside! Hut, two, three, four." And, sure enough, the Pigs were filing back into their room to view our afternoon mud bath. R.X. was gone.

Near the swimming pool a motel security guard with a two-way radio was shooing soccer kids away from the wedding. I grabbed Nick and Marshall, and we dropped back deeper into the small palm forest.

"Young men," a voice called. I was about to explain that we were just shy wedding guests, when it went on more quietly, "Excuse me, young Zappers." We all knew who *that* voice belonged to.

"Race you to the game room," Nick said, and he and Marshall ran. Chickens. I would have run with them, but the old guy looked so sad with his detective hat on. It was tilted sideways. He didn't look as though he was ever going to solve anything.

"Is this wedding a clue?" he asked me.

I didn't know. "Pretty expensive clue," I told him.

"Yes, I guess you're right. From what I know about W.O.R.M., they couldn't afford it. Those silver balloons must have cost a couple of dollars each. The only thing that makes me wonder is the ice. That big ice sculpture. I can't figure out what it is. It looks to me like a half-moon and a sun. If that's a clue, I don't understand it. They've told us that the murder had something to do with ice. And that's such *big* ice."

"Listen, I've got to go," I told him, but I wasn't in any real hurry. I was watching as the motel security man stopped Molly and Lisa from getting to the bride and groom. Molly had her hands on her hips. She was arguing. The motel man was shaking his finger at her.

"I know it wouldn't be fair for you to say anything more than you already have." The man tipped his detective hat back, took out a handkerchief, and wiped his forehead. "Let me explain what I know, and you tell me if it's right."

The security man was headed our way, so I nodded. Maybe I wouldn't look like a wedding gawker.

"All right, to start with, just after you left our meeting room, at two o'clock this afternoon, there was a heated argument between two actors. That set up the mystery. They're called, for the purpose of this game, Vic Tim and Ima Meany."

"Clever names," I told him.

"That's right," he said, laughing. "Like Zapper. In any case, Vic Tim was a motel inspector. Ima Meany was the motel manager. And then another actor argued with both of them. His name was Rex Suspect. Rex was supposed to own several motels, including this one. Am I confusing you?"

I thought about it. "No, Vic Tim is fighting with Ima Meany and Rex Suspect. It sounds like a cartoon."

"It does, doesn't it?" he replied. "Vic Tim said he'd found some ice that could get Ima fired and put Rex out of business. He said he'd tell the police unless they gave him money."

"Then Vic Tim gets killed. Right?"

"Right. It was such a shame. We'd all enjoyed a lavish lunch together. The chef even came. He carved a fine little ice figure for us with a power saw. Splendid fellow. But tell me, did you do it?"

"Wait a minute," I said. "With all those great suspects, how could you think it was me?"

"They were such bad actors," he said. "But when you ran out of there saying you were going to kill someone, you were quite believable."

The hotel security man passed us by. At least I looked innocent to him. I started to leave.

"You can't help, then?" the old man asked. "I don't seem to make head or tail of this. Do you think the lost necklace is a part of it?" He sighed. "I don't know—missing jewelry, a strange murder, meaningless clues, they don't add up. While

I do enjoy losing myself in a good mystery novel, I'm absolutely out of my depth here."

"If I could, I'd help," I told him. "There's no way I can, though. All I can say is good luck, Mr. . . ."

"Crook," he said. "Al Crook."

"You're kidding."

"No, it's true. Albert T. Crook, the third. I'm from a long line of Crooks, all of us law abiding. Both of my sons and all three of my splendid grandchildren are, of course, Crooks."

"They must get teased in school."

"Ah, yes," he said, "and so did I. The name is an easy mark." He shook his head. "Young Zapper, I'm beginning to think you really didn't do it."

"Mr. Crook," I told him, "I never said I did. My name isn't Zapper. It's Hobie Hanson. My team is the Zappers. I'm just a kid at a big soccer tournament. If you don't believe me you can ask my coach, Mr. Star. He's staying with us in room 306. I don't know anything about mysteries, but, listen, I'll do what I can." I lied, of course. How could I help?

Across the room Mr. and Mrs. Funny Face were feeding each other wobbly orange *Z*'s. All of the other soccer kids had been swept away.

With my muddy hair and grassy elbows, getting a good close look at them wasn't going to be all that easy, but since Molly and Lisa couldn't do it, I really wanted to try.

"So long," I said, and I'd walked about three steps when the security man who'd been making the rounds spotted me.

"Little boy," he said. "This is a private party. You are not invited."

I hate it when people call me little boy. "Big man," I told him. "Clowns like little boys. I'd make them laugh."

He did not smile. I could just hear my dad telling me I was asking for trouble. "Scoot," the guy said.

Mr. Crook was watching. I wandered back. "I didn't want to ruin anything," I told him. "I just wanted to look at those shoes, say hello, and find out what the blue ice thing is supposed to be, you know."

We stood and watched from the sidelines. A silver balloon floated up to the ceiling.

"If you really want to get closer, I could lend you my detective hat. They might think you're in costume, too," Mr. Crook said. The hotel man was standing by the golf course keeping his eye on me, though, so I couldn't chance it.

"Excuse me, sir," a soft voice behind us said. It was a tall guy wearing a big raincoat with the collar turned up. Very suspicious. "I wonder, sir, if you could do us a favor," he went on, glancing from side to side to see if anyone was watching. "The young man seems to be just the right size," he said, looking at me. "I wonder," he asked Mr. Crook, "if you would let us borrow your grandson?"

9. Beep! Beep! Beep!

"You want to borrow my grandson?" Mr. Crook said. "But Hobie's not . . ."

"You see, he's just the right height," the man in the raincoat said, sizing me up, "and the surprise won't work unless . . . I'd better explain," he went on, still talking soft, but really fast. "There are fourteen of us, all friends of Fred and Fiona."

"Fred and Fiona?" Mr. Crook asked. He took his hat off and ran his hand through his gray hair. "And they are . . . ?" You could see him trying to figure this out, trying to make it fit in the Who Dun It puzzle.

"Fred and Fiona Zemek. They're the bride and groom," the raincoat man said, nodding toward the wedding party. "All of us just graduated with them from Klown Kollege, and we came up to surprise them at their wedding."

The lady from bookkeeping knew what she was talking about. Still, this guy didn't much look like a clown.

"That's most thoughtful of you," Mr. Crook said, "but—"

"What have *I* got to do with it?" I asked the guy.

"Well, that's the thing of it. The next step in the surprise is getting in the car."

"Car?" Mr. Crook asked. "Are you leaving, then? Surely you don't expect Hobie to leave with you?"

"Oh, no, no," the guy said. "The car is a super-subcompact clown car we brought with us. We towed it all the way from Florida on a U-Haul trailer. It's over there behind those double doors in a staging area. What's going to happen is that thirteen of us will stuff ourselves inside the car and then drive right up to the wedding party, pop out one after the other, and knock the socks off Fred and Fiona."

"Will the security man let you?" I looked over, but the guy with the two-way radio had disappeared.

"No problem. We cleared it with him."

"Why do you want Hobie?" Mr. Crook asked.

"If he holds on tight he won't get hurt," the raincoat guy said. He turned his back to the wedding party. "Look, if Fred and Fiona see me, it will ruin the whole thing. The problem is that only thirteen of us are ready to go. The clown who always opens the car door got stomach flu at the last second, and she's upstairs being sick. She's short, just your grandson's size."

"But," Mr. Crook protested, "he's not—"

"Really, all he'll have to do is slip on the costume, roll in with us, slide off the car when it stops, and then open the door so we can all pile out. We need somebody to open the door from the outside. Don't worry about your grandson. He'll have a fine time. What do you say?"

It would be a *real* blast to ride on a clown car. What's more, it sounded safe. I mean, everybody else was a grown-up. What could possibly go wrong?

"Grandfather," I said to Mr. Crook, "dear Grandfather, if you let me do this, on my honor I promise to do my best to find out what happened to poor old Mr. Tim." I glanced up to see if any of the kids were watching me. Nobody was on the balcony.

"Let me just introduce you. Both of you, come with me." The raincoat guy headed toward the double door. "Come meet the others. You'll see." As he walked I could see his purple polka-dot pants. I ran after him, and Mr. Crook followed.

Behind the double doors, in a kind of warehouse room, a dozen clowns and a tiny silver car were waiting. The clowns were dressed in frizzy rainbow wigs, sparkle hats, yellow plaid pants, black-and-white crooked ties that almost reached the floor, all kinds of crazy stuff. Lots of them had happy faces painted on, but none of them was really smiling—until they saw me.

When the guy who'd talked to us said, "I found him, and he's just right!" they all whooped. He began at once to fasten a purple ball on his nose. Then he whipped his raincoat off. His shirt had purple polka dots on it, too.

A tall, thin clown in a black top hat stepped forward. "You're exactly right," he said to me.

"You're a lifesaver." Then he looked a little closer. "Your face and neck are a tad dirty, but I guess the costume will hide that."

"I'm sorry. I was playing soccer," I explained. "Today. In the mud."

"Boys will be boys," Mr. Crook put in, like he was apologizing for his messy grandson.

"Makeup should help," a clown in gold tights said. She came toward me with a jar of something yellow and a jar of something black.

Mr. Crook hadn't told them I could do it. I hadn't told them I would do it. But somehow, I was going to do it—whatever *it* was.

Clowns of all sizes and shapes were starting to pile into the baby-size silver car, which clearly wasn't big enough to hold all of them. Clearly. But they flattened their costumes down and, one-by-one, climbed in and fitted themselves together like spoons.

Before he got in, a clown in stripes winked at me and said, "I've got a closed umbrella frame in my coat. When I get out, I'll raise my arms, it'll open up, and I'll look as big as a blimp. You watch."

Still, it didn't seem possible. It was just the shell of a car. There weren't any seats inside.

There wasn't anything inside that I could see, except the stacked-up clowns and a small, dressed-up driver at the steering wheel.

"I'm Joe," the clown in the top hat said. "You work with me. Here's your suit. It zips all the way up the front."

The suit was black and white and fuzzy all over. I was sure I knew what it was. "It's a skunk suit," I said. "Do I have to spray or something?"

"Ed didn't explain?" he asked. "No? Well, in about two minutes all thirteen of us will be packed in the car. Go ahead, you step into your suit. It's not a skunk, I guarantee. And then put on the shoes. The costume isn't right without them." The shoes looked like swimming flippers, only they were black and yellow. "You can leave yours here," he continued. "Please hurry."

"But what is Hobie supposed to *do*?" Mr. Crook asked. As I took my shoes off, he picked them up and put one in each of his jacket pockets. It looked a little strange. "I feel responsible."

As I stepped into the costume I saw that the white part was in front. So I couldn't be a skunk. The black part in back was padded, and a black hood thing fit over my head. The arms were kind of wings. I flapped them.

"Do hold still," the woman in the gold tights said. She painted a black circle around each of my eyes and put some yellow on my nose. "There, that'll have to do," she said. "You look like an almost proper penguin."

A penguin! There weren't any mirrors, so I couldn't see myself, but I could feel I was a penguin. I slipped on the flippers. They were a little snug. Quack. Do penguins, I wondered, say quack?

The gold clown shoehorned her way into the wedge of space that was left. Now all of the clowns, except Joe in the top hat, were packed in tight and ready to go. And I'd thought we were crowded in Mrs. Rossi's van.

Joe hoisted me up to the very top of the car. "There are handles on each side so you can hold on. See them?" I sat down with my legs and finned feet hanging over the windshield. The black fuzzy wings lapped over the tops of my hands, but I held on tight.

"Now, we'll drive in with the horn honking," Joe went on. "Don't let go to wave or scratch or anything. It's slippery up there. The second we stop, you slide straight down the windshield and hood, waddle over to the car door, and open it

up. When I get out, you bow to me. Low. Got it?"

Hold on, slide down, waddle over, open door, bow low. I nodded. I wasn't up to talking.

"Keep holding the door open until everybody is out. Got it?"

I nodded again.

"Sir," Joe said to Mr. Crook, "while I crawl into the car, will you swing open those doors that lead into the atrium?"

Mr. Crook was standing there with his head in his hands, probably wondering who was going to sue him when I got killed. But he did what he was told. He ran over to the big double doors and he flung them wide.

The engine on the car under me started. The horn began to beep, a toy-car, high-pitched *beep-beep-beep,* and then, with a start, we began to move toward the atrium.

I suddenly felt funny. I was scared. I didn't know if it was because I was afraid I might fall off or because I might, just might, be doing one of those stupid things I wasn't supposed to do. My dad had said to keep my nose clean—and my nose was painted yellow.

10. Make Way for the Clowns

"All right, all right, folks. Outta the way, people. Outta the way. Make way for the clowns." It was the guy from motel security who'd chased me away from the wedding party. Now he was pushing people aside so I could get in. He should have been wearing a fancy uniform with gold braids. He should have been waving a baton and shouting, "La-a-adies and gen-n-ntlemen and chil-l-ldren of all a-a-ages . . ."

The piano player at the wedding must have been in on it, too, because as soon as we tooled out, she switched from whatever song she was playing to "If You're Happy and You Know It, Clap Your Hands." People all around started singing it and clapping.

Looking up, I could see fingers pointing down at me from the balconies. Little kids were squealing. Whole soccer teams who'd been hanging around the edges of the atrium cruising for something to do found me and yelled. But they didn't know who I was. They thought I was a fat, fuzzy, real penguin clown. The security guy kept shouting, "Make way for the clowns," and I was the only clown in sight.

The lady from bookkeeping was there with her friend, waiting. "See, I told you they'd be coming out. I was *in* on it all," she shouted. "Hi, Pengie! Hi, Clownie!" She waved, not knowing that just minutes before she'd told me I had dirty ears. Even her friend smiled. People were pressing in, calling and waving.

I wanted to wave back. I wanted to let loose and flap my wings, but Joe had warned me to hang on. I figured if I did let go, I'd slide down the hood when we screeched around the miniature golf course, and I'd end up as road kill.

"Quack," I yelled, instead of waving. "Quack."

I didn't see him, but I hoped Toby was watching. I hoped *everybody* was watching.

The car bounced to a stop about four feet from the bride and groom. If we'd bounced a couple more times we'd have bumped them both into the swimming pool.

Fiona, the bride, had taken off her rubber nose and red wig. Fred, the groom, had washed most of the green grin off his face, but he was still wearing the huge shoes. They both were just about hysterical when they saw the car. Fiona was jumping up and down. I don't think Fred could jump. His shoes were too big. He was holding onto his chest, though, like he thought his heart was going to pop out.

"Mimsy!" the bride yelled. "Mimsy, it's you!"

When the car stopped, I let go, took a deep breath, raised my wings, and slid as fast as I could straight down the windshield and hood. As soon as my feet hit the ground, a fountain of water squirted up behind me from where a hood ornament should have been. I'd just missed getting it.

The crowd went wild. Nobody ever yelled so loud for me in my whole life. Not even that one time I kicked in the winning goal in the last seconds of the game. I pulled my wings back and bowed. This was good. I wished my dad was here. He would love this.

"Mimsy," the bride called again. She hugged me. "You came, after all!"

She was squeezing me like toothpaste. I couldn't get loose. I couldn't catch my breath to say "I'm *not* Mimsy." All I could think of was that Joe was going to kill me if I didn't get him out of that car. Or they'd all die of suffocation. I could see those thirteen clowns packed in like pencils in a pencil box. I broke away from Fiona as fast as I could, without explaining that I was really Hobie Hanson, clown sub.

I started to run toward the car door. My feet wanted to run, but my flippers didn't. The first step I took, I tripped and fell flat on the fake grass. Everybody laughed. I went sliding across the slick plastic green. The crowd screamed. Four whole stories of people were breaking up over me falling on my face. My chin hurt.

"Kid!" I heard Joe call from inside the car.

I couldn't get up. My feet and the floppy costume kept getting in the way, so I crawled to the car door and opened it while I was on my knees. The people were laughing like maniacs.

The second I turned the handle, Joe stepped out with his black top hat, looking like he was going to a fancy ball with a princess, except he had a clown face on. I was still on my knees, so I bowed down till my head touched the grass.

Everybody laughed some more. Fiona ran to Joe. He picked her up and spun her around in the air.

And then all of the clowns stepped out, one by one by one. The clown in gold tights did sommersaults and flips. Sure enough, the guy in stripes raised his arms just as he got out, and his suit ballooned around him. It looked as though he'd taken *all* the space in the car himself. You could hear people suck in their breath. They couldn't believe it.

I could hardly believe it either, but the clowns kept coming. I could see them rolling out of their squashed places inside and then stepping out big. If I hadn't known better, I'd have thought there was a trap door. It was like where they'd come from they'd had all the room in the world.

The last clown out opened up a huge bass drum. Then he marched around banging it like thunder.

The crowd was even bigger now, yelling and

screaming. Up above, people were tearing newspapers into tiny bits and tossing them down like confetti. Kids from all sides were streaming into the party. Things were out of control.

The security guy was waving his arms. He seemed to be crying.

I grabbed the door handle and pulled myself up to my feet in time to see what looked like a parade. First came the guy with the big bass drum. He was pounding away and kicking his heels up high. Then came the bride waving her pink bouquet, the groom with his pancake shoes, and the rest of the clowns, clowning around. All of the other wedding guests just stood and stared, not able to even guess what would happen next.

The parade stopped at a big round table away from the swimming pool. It was covered with a pink cloth. In the middle of it was a wedding cake with two plastic clowns on top.

The clown in the purple polka-dot suit stepped forward and threw a purple polka-dot scarf high into the air. When it came down he flipped it away and there in the palm of his hand was a pigeon. It looked real, but it was a windup kind. He flung it high, and the pigeon flapped in big wide swoops, up toward the top of the Megadome. The crowd screamed and yelled and clapped.

Then the clown in stripes flung a silver scarf into the air, and when it settled in his hand, there was a silver box with a big bow underneath it. He gave the box to the bride.

The polka-dot clown caught the pigeon when it whirled down and sat it on the groom's shoulder. Altogether, it was some surprise.

Nobody had told me what to do after I slid off the car and opened the door. Nobody was paying much attention to me. I didn't want to get in the way. While they fooled around with the cake, I figured I would get to the pool and take a look at the big blue ice sculpture, to see what it really was. That way I could let Mr. Crook know if it might be a clue in his mystery game.

Very carefully I lifted my feet up and very carefully I set my flippers down, watching them closely to see that I didn't trip myself and go skidding across the turf again.

I had waddled almost over to the table that held what was left of the shrimp and gooey pink sandwiches and stuff, when I heard this kid yelp. It was a yelp I knew well. It was a Toby yelp.

"Whoopeeee! I *said* it was a penguin! I *said*!" I couldn't see him, but I could hear him loud and clear. That kid is never, ever going to need a microphone.

"The bride and groom will now cut the cake," somebody announced, and a lot of people clapped. More newspaper confetti floated down.

"But I have to throw my bouquet first, don't I? Isn't this the right time?" the bride asked. Here she was, surrounded by a bunch of clowns who'd arrived in a trick car, and she was worried about doing the right thing.

"A *penguin*!" Toby yelled, and I could see him now. He was crawling through a forest of wedding-guest legs. I turned and backed up toward the table with the party food and the ice. It was easier to walk backward than forward.

"I know who gets the bouquet," the bride said. "I know exactly who will get married next. Where is she? Mimsy! Where are you, Mimsy?" The clowns were trying to tell her where Mimsy really was, but she wouldn't listen. She spotted me. I backed up some more. "Don't try to hide. I see you, Mimsy."

But she didn't see Mimsy. She saw me in Mimsy's penguin suit.

Toby was beginning to gallop. He was getting up steam. I could tell what was coming, and I wasn't steady enough on my webbed feet to do anything about it. He was going to tackle me.

At the same time, Fiona wound up this big bunch of pink flowers and long waving ribbons, aimed, and let them fly. Toby and the wedding bouquet were both heading straight at me.

11. Making a Big Splash

If I didn't catch the flowers they would land in the swimming pool. I sure didn't want them. The bride was trying to make everything be right, though. And somehow soggy roses wouldn't be right, even for a clown.

Everybody else seemed to want them. There must be something about flying flowers. As the bouquet arced up through the air, people all around reached out for it, but the roses kept heading for me. It was like Fiona had been in football training camp, not clown school. The flowers had eyes. They found me. They hit me square in the chest, and I wrapped my wings around them without thinking. If I hadn't been wearing flippers I could have run in for the touchdown.

I was just standing there clutching the bouquet when Toby got me.

"Penguin," he yelled. "I caught the penguin."

He was hugging my knees and pushing at the same time. Lots of people, mostly kids, still had their arms up high. They wanted the bouquet. I didn't. I had to get rid of it. I didn't want anybody saying I was going to be the next one married. Maybe if I threw it away, nobody would remember I'd ever *had* it. I tossed the flowers as far as I could, which, since I was throwing with one short wing, wasn't all that far. It was so close, in fact, that I saw who caught them. It was somebody I'd seen before. I couldn't remember where. The eyes looked familiar, but I couldn't place the face.

Actually, I didn't have much time to wonder. Toby was still hugging and still pushing. He was forcing me and my webbed feet back to the table. I looked behind me to see what I could do. What I saw was part of the wedding buffet. I saw a glass platter of orange Jell-O *Z*'s, a bunch of shrimp, and a bowl of macaroni with little green vegetables in it. And behind them I saw the pool. It looked very close. As I put my wings on the table to steady myself, I felt it slide.

Toby was pushing me, and I was pushing the table. I tried to dig my heels in, but my feet belonged to a penguin. They wouldn't work for me.

The table slipped off the fake grass and onto the tile deck around the pool. People were laughing because I was a clown, but their giggles were beginning to sound nervous.

I bet they weren't half as scared as I was. When the table hit the tile, its legs slipped even faster.

"Toby," I yelled, "Toby, cut it out!"

"He knows me," Toby yelled to the crowd. "The penguin knows my name!" He did not stop hugging. He did not stop pushing.

The table did not stop moving.

"Toby," his mother called. She was out there trying to capture him, but the crowd was bigger and stronger than she was. "Toby," she called again, "you stop pestering that clown this minute!"

The table behind me had almost reached the edge of the swimming pool.

"Toby, let go!" I pleaded.

"Hobie?" he asked. "Are you Hobie in there?" He jumped away like he'd just discovered I was a python, not a penguin.

The second he let go, I fell back, giving the table an extra shove. That spread of food was about to become a submarine unless I did something fast. And so, I reached behind me with my right flipper and yanked the closest corner of the table toward me. It moved about two inches. All that did, though, was shift the opposite corner two inches closer to disaster.

Things got quiet fast. People nearby stood still with their mouths open. My flippered feet were set, but the rest of me was leaning. I was about to take a backward dive into the drink.

It was happening in slow motion. My whole life didn't pass before my eyes, but I did suddenly remember being at the dentist's locked door. I did see myself plowing through wet cement. And I did realize in a flash that falling into a swimming pool with a bowl of macaroni was not what my dad meant when he warned me to keep my nose clean.

My feet were lifting off the ground. I was just about to think what life would be like without a bike and soccer when some guy practically flew head first out of the crowd. Before I could hold my breath to keep the pool from rushing into my nose, my feet stopped moving. This guy tackled two legs, one of mine and one of the table's.

"Lean forward," he said. I bowed. My knees were like rubber, but I flapped my wings and got my flippers flat on the ground again.

The bride, the groom, and the clowns were all running in my direction. I turned to face them.

A cheer started up for the person who had saved the day, who'd kept the table and me from taking a bath. It was a good thing, a very good thing. I waved one wing to my fans in the crowd and leaned down to say thanks to the guy. But as quick as it started, the cheering stopped, and I could hear people suck in their breath.

It was not quite a good thing. The guy had stopped the fall, but one table leg hung over the edge of the pool. The top was sitting at an angle and the stuff on it was beginning to slide.

The bride screamed. I didn't blame her. I wanted to scream. This was something to scream about. Everything was going to be ruined, and I didn't know what to do.

I couldn't reach the big bowls and platters of food, but I could get at the pink tablecloth under them. I grabbed it with both wings and yanked.

It worked, too. The tablecloth whipped off zip-zap, like I was a magician. Everything on top of it, though, kept right on going.

"Stop," I yelled, but the food didn't stop. Nothing was going to keep it from falling.

The first to splash down was the big blue ice thing. *Sloosh,* it jackknifed into the pool. The crowd gasped.

"Help!" I called, and that worked about as well as yelling stop.

The rest of the stuff tobogganed smoothly off the slope—the half-empty plate of orange Jell-O *Z*'s, the fruit salad, the silver tray of little round pink sandwiches, sausages wrapped in bread, what was left of the macaroni, the platter of fat shrimp, a basket of rolls. *Plop,* they all fell in.

The crowd began to laugh like crazy. I didn't. I wanted to cry.

"Hobie." The guy on the floor holding the table leg said, "Hobie, I'm extremely sorry. If I'd known it was going to turn out like this I would never ever have allowed you to be a penguin. Could I, uh, bother you to help me up? I'd like to survey the damage."

"Mr. Crook!" He'd lost his detective cap somewhere, but that's who it was, all right, lying flat on his belly on the swimming-pool deck.

Joe, still wearing his top hat, and the clown in gold tights moved right in and lifted the table up from the brink.

I reached my hand down and helped Mr. Crook up. "You shouldn't have done that," I told him. "You're seventy years old."

"I tend to forget," he said, and he stood up, smiling. "I did it, though, didn't I?"

"You saved the day," I told him. "Your children and your children's children will be proud."

He looked down into the water and shook his head.

Most of the crowd was moving away now, making space between them and the mess. They were sure, you could tell, that this had stopped being funny.

Mr. Crook hadn't saved the day. He'd only saved the table—and me. The fruit salad was drifting into the middle of the pool, the sausages and the bowl of macaroni were sinking, and the Jell-O *Z*'s were dissolving into orange polka dots. The blue ice, though, looked at home. So did the shrimp.

I wished I was at home. If they called the police on me, that would make it twice in two days. I was thinking about diving in to rescue the salad, when the bride and the groom came up and stood beside me. I closed my eyes. Maybe I would disappear.

"I always wanted my wedding to be a day to remember," Fiona said. I waited for her to tell me how I'd ruined it all. "I expect *you'll* remember it, too," she told me. And then she laughed. I couldn't believe it. The bride *laughed.* "What do you think, Fred? A proper wedding for a couple of proper clowns?"

"We'll remember every splash of it," the groom said, and he gave her a hug.

The bride was holding a pink napkin with a big slice of wedding cake on it. She gave it to me. It was chocolate.

"I'm not Mimsy," I told her.

"I guessed," she said, and staring down into the wedding soup, she giggled. I thought for a minute she was going to dive in and splash around with the shrimp just to prove that things really were okay.

Mr. Crook brushed off his clothes and

cleared his throat. "Excuse me, Mr. and Mrs. . . . uh . . . Clown," he began. "Let me offer my heartfelt congratulations and best wishes. It's a shame about the mishap. If there's anything I can do . . ."

He reached into his jacket pockets, took one shoe out of each, and handed them to me. "I'm sure I saw a suspicious-looking necklace go by," he whispered in my ear. "I'm going to investigate." He smiled at the bride.

"Thank you for coming," she said. "Somehow, I don't think it would have been the same without you." She patted me on the head like I was a puppy.

I tried not to look in the pool. "I don't know how much damage I did. I've got five dollars and fourteen cents," I said, even though I knew it was already in the cement fund.

Fred knelt down and lifted the floating tray of pink sandwiches out of the drink and onto the deck. As we watched, the fruit salad filled with warm pool water and the bowl sank slowly to the bottom. "We'd already eaten a lot of the food," he said. "Shouldn't amount to too much. Don't know how they'll lasso *that,* though." He nodded at the ice that was bobbing along, cooling the pool.

He said it shouldn't amount to too much. He didn't say it wouldn't amount to *anything*. Still, it didn't sound as though they were going to call the F.B.I., the police, or, worst of all, my parents. But then, of course, they thought my grandfather already knew. Maybe if I was nice, very, very nice, they'd forget about what I'd done. I took a deep breath.

"I wonder," I said, "can you tell me what that blue thing is supposed to be?"

Fred laughed. "You're not the first to ask," he said. "We ordered an ice sculpture for the table that would make people think 'circus.' And that's what the motel chef carved."

"It wasn't exactly what we had in mind, but he only charged us half the regular price," Fiona said. "He told us it was going to do double duty. It's supposed to be a performing seal."

The round part had come loose and was floating free. "The ball," she went on, "used to balance on its nose."

Sure enough, when you knew what it was, you could tell. It was a practically life-sized seal

playing in the water. Its left eye was sparkling like crazy in the light.

People were beginning to wander away. It was getting late. Mr. Star was probably having kittens. It was almost suppertime, and I was starving. Still, I had to set the piece of cake down on the empty table. Penguin clowns don't handle food very well.

I looked for Mr. Crook, but he was gone. I wanted to thank him, but he hadn't come back. He was probably trying to get as far away from me as he could. I couldn't blame him, either. I was trouble.

On the other side of the pool, the guy from the motel was standing with a net in his hand. I bet he'd never captured a seal with it before.

I better hurry, I thought, so he won't catch me. As quickly as I could, I pried off the flippers. Then, after lifting the hood from my head, I unzipped the penguin suit and stepped out. Joe was waiting for the costume. "I'm sorry I wrecked everything," I told him.

He shrugged. "Your grandfather stopped the table, at least. The seal probably likes it in there. At least it's got plenty to eat.

"You were a good clown," he went on. "The crowd thought you were funny. Keep it in mind when those grown-ups start asking you what you want to be when you grow up."

The wedding party moved away from the pool. Joe tipped his top hat to me and followed them.

Now that the crowd in the atrium was quiet, I could hear Toby shrieking somewhere out near the lobby. "It was *Hobie*!" he yelled. "Don't say no, it was! It was Hobie in the penguin. I could *tell.*"

When I got my shoes on and turned around to go, a bunch of soccer kids were standing near the pool. They looked at me once, and then they looked again. Even with the black eyes and painted yellow beak they realized who I was. I almost turned and dived into the pool when I saw who *they* were.

Nick was there and Marshall *and* R.X.

"I don't believe it," Nick said.

Marshall stared at me hard. "It can't be," he said, shaking his head.

R.X. laughed. "I always knew you were a clown."

"Hey, you guys, it's another Zipper," a kid called. Then I saw that some of the group were Pigs. One of them, I could now tell, was the Pigs' giant goalie, Magdalena. Magdalena was smiling at me big time. And she was hugging, really tight, the big bouquet of pink roses that I'd thrown straight into her arms.

I ran, and as I ran, I heard the security guy yell, "Hey, you, Penguin, who's gonna pay for this mess?"

12. Pranks a Lot

"So *that's* why you can't tell anybody the penguin was me," I explained to the guys. "First, I blow off the dentist, next my dad sees me riding no-hands through an intersection, and then yesterday I plow a canal through the sidewalk. And that's just *this* week. My dad would not think this is funny. Trust me. He would take away my bike, my soccer, and my personal freedom. He would ground me forever."

"Did you do the cement on purpose?" Nick asked me. He was laughing. He was breaking up. *He* could laugh. It hadn't happened to him. "The

Hobester," he said, "a cement-sicker once again. Cement sicker and sicker and sicker."

"It's *not* funny," I said. "That's exactly why I didn't tell you before. I knew you'd start calling me names and bugging me."

So then of course Nick had to tell them how when I was Toby's age that's what I called cement mixers. I stormed into the bathroom to take a shower. I had to scrub off all the soccer dirt, clown paint, and penguin fuzz.

"Hey, Hanson," R.X. called through the door, "did you call spaghetti 'piscetti,' too?"

"Cement-sicker!" I could hear them all singing over and over and laughing. Maybe, though, it would keep them quiet about the clown disaster.

When I got out of the shower they were watching TV. They were ready and waiting for Mr. Star so we could go eat.

"No more calling me names, okay?" I said. "I'm not laughing. Anyway, you've got better things to do than bug me."

R.X. grinned, and then he began to hum. And then he began to sing—loud—like we were second graders. "Hobie's got a *girl*friend."

"Cut it out," I told him.

". . . a girlfriend, a girlfriend. Hobie's got

a *girl*friend, who says he's cute, cute, cute."

"Enough," I said. "I'm one of the good guys, remember?" I turned the TV up. The six o'clock news was on. There was nothing about the wedding. Mostly people were crying about one thing or another. The clowns would have been better.

Marshall turned the TV down a couple of notches. "Actually," he told me, "what Magdalena said was that she thought you were the cutest stuffed penguin she ever saw. I don't, of course, know how many stuffed penguins she's seen."

Big joke. They could hardly stop laughing.

"That cake was very good." Nick picked a crumb off the pink napkin.

Good old Nick. He'd changed the subject. The cake *was* good. As soon as we got back to the room we'd broken the slice into fours. It had this really sweet raspberry filling and a thick pink icing with sugary flowers and leaves on it. We weren't sure if you were supposed to eat the flowers or not, but we did, and it hadn't killed us yet. I was still hungry, but the cake had helped.

"Will you and Magdalena have chocolate cake like that at your wedding?" Nick went on. "I mean, you *both* caught the same bouquet."

I narrowed my eyes at him.

"You think you'll wear the bird suit when you say 'I do'?" R.X. asked. "Magdalena would like that."

"Cut it *out*!" I yelled.

"Cut what out?" Mr. Star asked, as he opened the door.

"Nothing," I said. "Just a friendly conversation."

His arms were full of clothes. "Well," he sighed, "I'm glad to be back. I had a long wait at the local Laundromat. A lot of other coaches had the same idea. We had a good time, though. Mostly we talked soccer strategy. Like how much bleach to use." He dropped the clean uniforms on a bed. "And you?" he asked. "What did you boys do with the rest of the afternoon?"

"Not much," I told him.

"I hope you didn't sit up here and watch television," he said.

"Oh, no," R.X. began, "we just turned it on. Actually, we did lots of interesting things." He grinned. "While I was taking a shower the rest of the guys went down to . . ."

". . . to watch a wedding party that was going on right out in the open in the atrium," Nick said.

"I mean, we didn't barge in at all, we . . ."

"We cruised around and then we came back up to get R.X.," Marshall explained. "His aunt, we found out, gave him ten dollars for his birthday . . ."

"One dollar for each year," R.X. said. "And we changed it all into tokens, and, for a while there, we ruled the game room."

"I got eighty-seven thousand points on—" Nick was saying, when Mr. Star cut him off.

"That's not much better than watching television," he told us, "but at least you didn't get into trouble."

"Right," I said. "No trouble. Absolutely not."

The phone rang. Mr. Star picked it up. He listened for a while and then he said, "Young lady, you have the wrong number. I don't think you need to call this room again."

"What did the young lady want?" R.X. asked him.

"A prank call," Mr. Star told him. "Someone whose name, she said, was Magdalena, was asking to talk to somebody she called Penguin."

R.X., Marshall, and Nick broke up.

"Oh, look, everybody," I said, "these people on TV are talking about foreign trade." I sat down and stared at the set. I could feel my ears turn red.

"When they get away from home," Mr. Star told us, "some children just don't know how to act properly. They make prank phone calls like that, run up and down the halls, stay up late at night interrupting everybody's sleep, and, in general, see how much they can get away with. It's immature."

"It's disgraceful," Nick said, and he smiled.

"Bad," we all agreed.

"Anybody in my group of players who doesn't know how to behave gets barred from tomorrow's game, that's for sure," Mr. Star went on.

"Absolutely," R.X. said, standing behind Mr. Star, flapping his elbows at me like they were wings.

The phone rang again. "Hello," Mr. Star said sharply, like he was really going to chew out whoever was on the other end. "Oh, hello, Mrs. Rossi. Yes, we're ready. We're going to meet downstairs in the coffee shop in"—he looked at his watch—"ten minutes. Oh, sure, you go ahead. I expect your little boy's hungry." Mrs. Rossi and Toby had a room of their own. At least we didn't have to sleep in the same space with the kid. Mr. Star was bad enough.

There was a knock on the door.

"Get it, will you, Hobie?" Mr. Star asked. "Probably it's one of the boys from Mr. Cabell's group. They're in room 206, just below us. When I stopped by with the uniforms, they were watching our game video. No pretty picture that. Doubtless they're starving."

I wasn't starving anymore. My stomach felt funny. Nobody in the hall was starving, either. Nobody was in the hall. I looked both ways.

Then I looked down. On the floor there was one pink rose.

If Nick saw it I'd never live it down. I might as well run away from home. I stuffed it in my jeans pocket and closed the door. "It was a joke knock," I said.

"See, that's exactly the kind of thing I mean," Mr. Star told us. "Some children just can't handle it. Let's go. We'll walk down the steps. I don't know why, but the elevators in this place always seem to be busy."

"Elevator tag," Marshall whispered as we started out.

"Remember," Nick whispered back. "When we play at midnight, you're It."

As our door was about to slam, the telephone rang again.

"I'll get it," I said. "You guys go ahead." If it was Magdalena, I was going to tell her to stop calling and quit leaving roses at my door. This was embarassing.

"Hobie," the voice on the phone said. "I'm so glad I caught you. I hope you're all right." It was Mr. Crook. "I'm sorry to have left so abruptly, but I had some serious sleuthing to do. I found out one thing for certain. The chocolate cake Vic Tim ate *was* poisoned. I was right. That's how the murderer did it."

"I'm okay," I told him. "I got some wedding cake. It was chocolate, too." Wait a minute, I thought. *I* had just had a big chunk of that cake. What if the sick feeling in the pit of my stomach was poison? And then I remembered that it was a fake murder and fake poisoned cake and the sick feeling was that somehow I just couldn't seem to stay out of trouble. "How are *you* doing?"

"I'm progressing," he said.

"Congratulations," I told him. "Listen, I've got to . . ."

"Hobie," he went on, "I still don't know who did it. There's at least one missing clue I need before the big Who Dun It banquet. It's at midnight." He laughed. "That's well after my usual bedtime."

"Mine, too. Mr. Crook, I . . ."

"Now it's possible," he said, "that one of the others has it. They *say* they don't. I'm *sure* it has something to do with the third floor ice-making machine where they found Vic Tim. It's near you. If you could—"

"Mr. Crook," I told him. "I've got to go eat."

"Just one minute more. The people in charge of the Who Dun It murder seem to be angry with you."

"With me? You're kidding." That's all I needed, more people mad at me.

"Not exactly with you. With the penguin. They say he ruined things. I can't figure that one out. The wedding seemed genuine enough, didn't it? Fred and Fiona certainly were." He sighed. "Perhaps I should give up and get a good night's sleep. I just hate to disappoint my grandchildren. You know? They were so pleased to have thought of this weekend. I wanted to please them back by solving the mystery."

"Mr. Crook, I'm sorry. The team's waiting for me in the coffee shop."

The phone went quiet. "Of course," he said. "I do apologize. I don't know what I was thinking. It's my problem. Besides, it's not at all important. It's just a game. Have a pleasant supper. I hope that tomorrow your team triumphs. Knock them dead—so to speak."

"Thanks. Thanks for everything. Well, goodbye," I told him, and then I hung up.

He was a nice old man, but there wasn't any way I could help him. How was I going to dig up a clue before midnight? If it was a cube of ice it would have melted. Even the big ice seal was much thinner. We'd stood on the balcony to eat our cake and watched some guys pull the seal out. They raised it with a net and left it on a beach towel by the side of the pool.

I felt bad, though. Mr. Crook had dived across the fake grass to save the table and my penguin. He risked his seventy-year-old bones for me. No way I could have swum in that suit. I'd have sunk straight to the bottom.

I had told Mr. Crook that if he would let me be a clown, on my honor I'd help him solve his mystery. On the other hand, I'd told my dad that I would absolutely, positively not get into any trouble. Somehow, I'd gotten into a lot, and prowling the halls looking for murder clues sounded as though it could get me into a whole lot more.

As I was walking out the door, the phone rang again. I started back, but then I decided to let it ring. It was probably just a joke call.

13. Power Punch

Toby was sitting in a booster chair at a table with his mother and four girls from the team. He had ketchup in his hair and a hot dog in his mouth. When he took it out, his mouth was full of bun, but he said, anyway, "That was you before, wasn't it?"

"*This* is me now," I told him, and I escaped as fast as I could.

"Penguin!" he yelled, but I was already across the coffee shop to where the rest of the team was sitting at two big tables. Mr. Cabell was at one. Mr. Star was at the other. The rest of the guys from 306 were at Mr. Star's table. So were Molly and Lisa.

As I got there, a waitperson was already taking their orders. "Okay," she said, "I've got five bacon burgers, five cheese fries, four chocolate fudge malts, and one cherry root beer. Right?"

"Cherry root beer?" I asked as I sat down next to Nick.

"That's mine," R.X. told me. "It sounded good. What took you?"

"Nothing," I told him. "Can I have the same burger, fries, and malt as the others?" I asked the waitperson. "Hold the cherry root beer."

"You got it," she said. "And you, sir?"

"Well, that sounds a bit rich to me. How about, oh . . . What if I just order"—Mr. Star lowered his voice, like he thought maybe only she would hear—"the Megadome Slimtrim Special and skim milk."

"Mr. Star," Molly asked, "are you on a diet?"

He shrugged. "Well, not really. It's only that, except for its silly name, the Slimtrim Special sounds absolutely delicious. It's been a long time since I had poached fish, nonfat cottage cheese, and steamed vegetables without butter. Besides, I haven't been getting much exercise lately, and

I do seem to have put on a few inches around my waist."

"So you *are* on a diet," R.X. said. "Well, that's good to know. We'll all help. We'll keep an eye on you to make sure you don't cheat. No more bags of Tootsie Rolls, right?"

We all agreed to help. Mr. Star did not look pleased.

Molly stood up. "I would like to take this opportunity, while we wait for our food, to make a presentation."

She was talking loud. People at other tables turned to look. Molly waved across the room, and Mrs. Rossi and the girls sitting with her waved back. Toby stuck out his tongue. Behind them a bunch of the Pig team was sitting in a booth. Quint was there. So was Magdalena. She waved. I slid down in my seat.

Molly reached under our table and pulled out a striped box tied with a red bow.

It was the coach's gift. Every year the team that gets to go to the tournament gives its coach a gift. Molly had collected two dollars from everybody, and her grandmother had gone out and bought a present, so that's why Molly was doing the talking.

"Mr. Star," she said, "we may not be the best team here, but we think you're the best coach ever." Lisa clapped. "And we hope if they ask you to coach soccer again next year, you won't get cold feet." Lisa clapped again. Molly seemed to be finished, so, even though it was a kind of lame talk, we all clapped with her.

Mr. Star stood up. "Well," he said, "it's been my pleasure. You played hard today, and I know you will tomorrow, too. And I want you to know that I'm proud that you're behaving yourselves so well. You're being very mature."

Nick made a face at me. I made one back.

Mr. Star shook the box. "Will anything jump out and snap at my nose?"

"No," Molly told him, "it's not silly. It's a useful gift. And it's not anything that will make you fatter, either."

Mr. Star looked a little less pleased, but he pulled off the ribbon, unfastened the striped paper, and started to take off the lid. "Ready?" he asked.

He lifted the lid, looked inside, and stared for a full minute before he said, "Wow. I mean, wow, that's really . . . I see what you mean about not getting cold feet. These are certainly . . .

something." Reaching in, he lifted out what looked like a pair of fuzzy black and white soccer balls. I thought maybe they were pillows that Molly wanted him to put on his living-room sofa. But they weren't pillows. They were enormous bedroom slippers. The tops were the size of a real soccer ball cut in half, and they were made of the same soft, plushy cloth as a baby's stuffed bear.

"The store also had slippers that looked like basketballs and footballs," Molly told him, "but my grandmother thought these would be more appropriate."

"Oh, yes," he said. "My, yes."

"Put them on," Lisa told him. Mr. Star turned pale.

"And they look a lot more cozy than, for instance, penguin flippers," R.X. said.

I kicked him under the table.

"Do put them on," Molly begged.

"Not while we're eating," Mr. Star said. "Later. Later I'll model them for you." I bet he hoped we'd all forget.

Our drinks came, and we started in. First, we tore open the wrappers around our straws, twisted the ends nice and tight, and then blew the wrappers across the room.

"Boys," Mr. Star warned us. "That's enough of that," which wasn't fair because Molly and Lisa did it, too. Then he got up to show the slippers to Mr. Cabell.

"Yuck," R.X. said. "This cherry root beer is revolting. It's disgusting. It's gross enough to make you lose your appetite."

"Maybe you should give it to Mr. Star. He doesn't want an appetite," Marshall suggested.

"It'd probably work even better if we made it into Power Punch," Nick said.

Mr. Star had gone to Mrs. Rossi's table to show the soccer slippers to the kids there.

"Okay, Power Punch for Mr. Star," R.X. agreed. "Everybody has to put one thing in. And everybody's got to taste it." He reached over and picked up a shaker. "To the cherry root beer, I will add a little pepper." He shook some in. Then he tasted it, made a face, and passed the glass to me.

"To the cherry root beer and pepper, I will add Tabasco sauce." I took a bottle of it from a tray in the middle of the table and shook two red drops into the glass. I watched them float toward the bottom, and before they could dissolve, I sipped a little and passed the glass to Nick. The cherry root beer part tasted worse than the pepper.

"To the cherry root beer, pepper, and Tabasco, I will add a small spoonful of sugar," he said. He did, and it fizzed. He licked the foam on top.

"Sugar was cheating," Molly said, and she put in pickle relish. "It's not bad," she told us.

Lisa added Sweet 'n Low, but refused to taste it.

Marshall stirred in "a hint of mustard." He took a sip. "It tastes like somebody dropped in a hot dog with all the works."

That got it back to R.X. "Except we forgot the ketchup," he said, and he gave it a squirt. Just as he put it down, Mr. Star and our waitperson both arrived.

Our meals were excellent. We added so much mustard and ketchup and pickle relish to the hamburgers that they oozed over the sides of the buns. The fries were crisp and the cheese on top was warm and drippy so you could lick it off your fingers. The malt was like frozen fudge. It was the best meal I ever ate.

Mr. Star kind of picked at his brussels sprouts.

"Don't you like them?" Lisa asked him.

"Oh, they're fine. Fine. Very tasty. Just a little cold. Not exactly cold. More like tepid."

"Well," Molly told him, "you ought to send them back. My grandmother sends things back all the time."

He cut a piece of pale fish, dashed it with Tabasco, and ate it. "It's fine. Tell me, R.X., how is the cherry root beer? I've never heard of putting cherry flavoring in root beer."

R.X. grinned. "It's an old family favorite," he said. "You want a taste?" He stirred the Power Punch and scooped out a spoonful for Mr. Star. "Try it," he said. "You'll like it."

Mr. Star took the spoon. We all watched closely as he smelled the punch and wrinkled his nose. Then, looking R.X. in the eye, he sipped a little. "Curious," he said. He hadn't swallowed it down in a gulp, just *tasted* it. Then he smiled. "R.X.," he said, "I wouldn't want to take away one drop more of your favorite drink. For myself, I think I'll just stick to milk."

R.X. raised the glass and was about to chug it totally down, I know he was. It's something R.X. would do. Only that's when Quint came up to the table.

"So, R.X.," he said, "that was some game of catch."

"Sure was," R.X. said, looking nervous. He didn't want Mr. Star to find out he'd been out on the balcony throwing a ball at somebody two rooms away. "You want some cherry root beer?"

"No, thanks." Quint made a weird face. "It sounds disgusting."

"It is," I said. "Who do you play tomorrow?"

Quint grinned. He knew we were trying to change the subject. He could have told on R.X., but he didn't. He could also tell on me. "We play the Gazelles. They're good. Not as good as we are, of course, but good."

As he started to leave, he turned back and looked at me. "By the way, I promised to tell you that Magdalena says hi." He gave me the old lip curl. "Good luck tomorrow. You're going to need it." And off he went.

"What was that all about?" Molly asked. "When were you playing catch with him, R.X.? And who's Magdalena?"

I shrugged.

R.X. shrugged.

"It's pushing toward eight o'clock," Mr. Star told us. "While I pay the bill here, you go ahead upstairs. At 8:30 I want the girls to come to room 306 so that those of us who haven't seen it can take a look at the game video. You can learn a lot by watching yourselves play a difficult opponent."

We all groaned. We didn't need to watch to know how bad we'd been.

At the next table Mr. Cabell laughed. "Don't

groan, you're going to love it. We did. It's a great film, if I do say so myself. Besides the game, which is certainly dirty, I got about twelve minutes of that crazy clown wedding reception. The penguin kept falling flat on his face. He was a riot. You're gonna love it."

14. Ice Scream

The video was all that Mr. Cabell had said it would be and worse. He'd caught me sticking my tongue out at the camera. He'd caught me missing the ball by a mile. More than once. He got Nick spraying Magdalena with mud. He got Lisa's cheer. He got every one of the Pigs' goals. Mr. Star sat in the only easy chair, wearing his big, fuzzy soccer slippers. As the video played, he gave us a lot of advice. We hadn't done a lot of zapping.

Kids were hanging out on the rug, the bed, all over. I was sitting cross-legged between the beds. When the wedding party came on, I was almost afraid to look, but the car really *was* funny. I was funny on top holding tight with both wings. When I fell down and crawled to the car door, it looked like a real clown gag. Nobody but R.X., Marshall, and Nick knew it was me, and I couldn't tell. It was too risky.

"Whoever would do such a thing?" Mr. Star asked. "I can't imagine why anybody in their right mind would want to have a wedding like that."

I almost told him, "It's Fred and Fiona. They went to Klown Kollege together, and they're nice, not weird. Not *very* weird." Maybe he wouldn't be mad I was there, after all. But then Mr. Cabell zoomed in close on the stuff crashing into the water, and I couldn't watch anymore. Closing my eyes wasn't enough. I stuck my head under the bed.

Whenever something more splashed into the pool, kids screamed louder.

"That ice thing," somebody said, "looks big enough to sink the Titanic."

"What are you doing under the bed, Hobie?" Aretha asked.

"Looking for something," I said, resting my ear

on the rug. I had to stay low because the kids on the bed were bouncing the springs when they laughed. I blinked till my eyes got used to the dark, and a bump on the rug turned out to be something real. Crawling almost all the way under, I grabbed it and pulled it to me.

I knew what it was. It was the small ball that Quint had kicked into the room when his coach caught them playing soccer in the hall. Maybe he wanted it back. As soon as I squeezed it, though, I could feel that it wasn't a ball. It was something hard wrapped in paper.

The game video was over.

"Hey, Hobie, you've got to come out now," Marshall told me. "You can run, but you can't hide. Mr. Star is going to show it one more time. He's going to tell us again what we did wrong."

"That's not true," Mr. Star said. "I'll help you decide for yourselves what you could have done differently."

I snaked back out, leaving whatever it was I'd found under the bed. Somehow, I didn't want to show it to everybody.

The game video was as bad the second time around as it was the first. Mr. Star kept pointing out what an excellent goalie Magdalena was. Every time he told us what she was doing right, R.X. sang, "Hobie's got a girlfriend," and he didn't stop until I punched him one.

"Enough of that scuffling, boys," Mr. Star said. "It's not funny. Neither is that falling-down clown business. I think we'll skip it this time." But everybody complained so much that he let it run. I watched until the disaster part, when I dived under the bed again.

I grabbed the fake ball. The paper around it was fastened on with rubber bands. It peeled right off. Something was written on the paper, but it was too dark to read, so I stuffed it in my pocket. What it had been wrapped around was smooth and plastic, just the right size to hold in my fist.

When the video stopped, somebody pulled off my shoes and my socks. Then they started tickling my feet. I had to drop the thing I'd found and wiggle myself out of there fast, kicking and yelling.

The girls were leaving. "I've got more writing to do," Molly explained. "I've decided that the team in my story will lose again. They will lose at the last second. It will be sad. Judges like sad, I think, more than happily ever after. It will be the goalie's fault that they lose. And the goalie"—she looked straight at me—"will be named Magdalena."

"It's almost nine," Aretha said. "That's my bedtime."

I didn't believe it. "Wait a minute, who's the adult person that's staying in the room with you?" I asked.

"Nobody," Lisa said.

"Nobody!"

"Mrs. Rossi is dropping in occasionally," Mr. Star explained, "to see if they need anything, but . . ."

"*We* are trustworthy," Molly said, looking smug. "And we're extremely tired." They were conning Mr. Star into believing they were sleepy, but they would be up practically all night long, yakking. Guaranteed.

"Unfair," Marshall said.

"Unfair," I agreed.

The girls yawned huge, extremely fake yawns. And then they left.

"Well," Mr. Star said when the door closed behind them, "I see by the schedule that there's a fine documentary on TV at nine o'clock. It's about termites. We can watch it together until 9:30 and then turn in. You must be as exhausted as the girls are. This has been one long day."

He sank down in the soft chair and bounced his soccer-ball feet together.

It wasn't going to do any good to complain. Mr. Star always does what he says he's going to. And that would include not letting us play the next day if he caught us breaking his rules.

The termite TV show was awful. It was so boring that it wasn't fair. I couldn't keep my eyes open. I wanted, almost more than anything, to put my head on a nice, soft pillow and go to sleep.

While Mr. Star was setting up his cot by the windows near the balcony, I went in the bathroom, locked the door, and splashed cold water on my face. I didn't much care about it anymore, but I reached in my pocket and pulled out the paper. When I opened it up, it tore on the creases, but I could still read what it said. On one side, somebody had scrawled in big, shaky red letters: S(T)EAL.

That didn't make any sense, so I turned it over. The other side was a kind of chart. At the top it said, "Ice Inspection Sheet." There were marks on it for different ice-making machines and how clean they were and how clear and whole their ice was.

It was the lost clue, lost under our bed. I hoped Mr. Crook would know what it meant. I didn't.

"Aren't you finished in there yet? Let me in!" R.X. was pounding on the bathroom door.

When I got back I found out that Nick and I had one bed and Marshall and R.X. the other. Everybody was ready to brush their teeth and turn in.

Nobody but Nick was looking when I reached under the bed and pulled out the plastic thing that had been wrapped in the paper. I'd thought it was a ball, but it looked exactly like an ice ball. It was a fake ice cube for a fake murder.

I cupped it in my hand and showed it to Nick, and then I put it in my pocket with the paper.

"So?" he asked.

"Remember the old guy in the detective hat?" I whispered. "His name is Mr. Crook. No kidding. Anyway, I'm just about positive this is a clue to his Who Dun It mystery. It was that ball thing that Quint kicked into the room, remember?"

He nodded. "If it's a clue, what's it mean?" he whispered back.

I shrugged, and then quick got under the covers with all my clothes on and pulled the blanket up to my neck. "I've got to get it to him before midnight. He's the one who saved me from falling in the pool. I owe him. Want to come along?"

He jumped in bed with his jeans on, too. "What if they catch us?" he asked. "If you think your dad is mad at you now . . ."

Mr. Star came out of the bathroom and turned out all the lights. You could still see, though. Light and music were both filtering in from the atrium. "Well, good night," he said, and climbed into his roll-away cot.

"Mr. Star?" Marshall asked.

"Yes, Marshall?"

"Mr. Star, do we know yet who we're playing tomorrow?"

Mr. Star yawned. "I hope I don't keep you boys awake with my snoring," he said, and then he yawned again. "Tomorrow. Yes. We play another team that lost today." There was a long pause. I thought he'd fallen asleep. "Strange team name. Seems to me I've heard it somewhere before. I can't imagine why they chose it. Couldn't possibly fit on their uniforms."

R.X. was snoring. The digital clock said ten-o-five, and R.X. was already sound asleep.

"Call themselves," Mr. Star said, "the Daring Devastators."

15. Who Dun It?

"Hobie!" Somebody was kicking me. I kicked back. "Hobie!" This time it was an elbow in the ribs.

"Huh?" I didn't know where I was. Where I wanted to be was back asleep.

"It's eleven-thirty."

"So?" I opened my eyes and looked at the clock on the table by the bed. Eleven-thirty. I had to be somewhere before twelve. Before twelve midnight. I didn't know where.

"I can forget it if you can," Nick was saying. "Except I'm wide awake. You wanted to take something to that guy."

"To my grandfather," I told him.

"No, wake up," he whispered, right in my ear. "To Mr. Crook."

When I blinked again, I realized who Mr. Crook was, but I wasn't sure *where* he was. I rolled out of bed and stood up. And then I remembered that he'd given me his room number when he thought *I* was a clue. I'd put it in my soccer pants.

Everybody else seemed sound asleep. I grabbed my duffel, took it into the bathroom, closed the door quietly, and flipped on the light. My pants were neatly folded. The note was still in the pocket. When I pulled it out, though, the paper crumbled in my hands. Whatever it said had been finished off by the bleach at the Laundromat. I didn't know where Mr. Crook was, and so I couldn't take him the clue.

I closed my eyes and yawned. I could get back in the warm, soft bed. That was okay. This was just a dumb game with joke ice and fake murders. It didn't matter, not to me, anyway. It wasn't my game. In my game you hit balls with your head.

I opened my eyes. No fair, I was waking up. I'd promised Mr. Crook I'd help. On my honor. And, weird as it was, he seemed to care a lot about which actor killed Vic Tim and what happened to some pretend diamond necklace. I could get up and help, but I'd promised my dad I'd absolutely, positively be on my best behavior.

I turned to the door, closed my eyes, and then opened them again. What if best behavior was stalking a fake killer with Mr. Crook?

Also, I'd told my Dad I would think before doing stuff. So I thought. I thought about putting the phone under the covers and calling the hotel desk. Maybe they'd give me Mr. Crook's number. If I did it very quietly, Mr. Star might not hear.

Brrrrrrring! A phone was ringing. *Our* phone was ringing. *Brrrrrrring!*

"Hello." Through the bathroom door I could hear Nick answer it. "Hello, who is this?"

"What?" Mr. Star asked.

"You guys, cut it out. There are people sleeping here," Nick said and hung up.

"What?" Mr. Star asked again. "Who was that?"

"Some kids singing," Nick told him. "They were wishing us good luck tomorrow. Sort of. I told them not to do it again."

Mr. Star was awake now. We'd never get out. My Mickey Mouse watch said eleven-thirty-five. I stood as quiet as I could and tried to think some more. My brain was working on low voltage. Mr. Crook. Clue. Midnight. Midnight banquet. Banquet! That's where he'd be. And the banquet would be at . . . The banquet would be in the room where I first saw him. I'd try there. As soon as I could, I'd get Nick, and we'd try there.

I turned off the bathroom light, opened the door carefully, and inched back into the bedroom.

"He's snoring again," Nick whispered. "You gonna do it?"

"Do what?" R.X. asked from his bed.

Three of us would be too many. I didn't want R.X. to come.

"I've got to meet somebody," I told him.

"You gonna sneak out?" he asked. "Who you gonna meet?"

"Somebody. But . . . but I don't know how we're going to get back in." This was true. "Mr. Star has the key. Can you sit by the door and let us in?"

"Us?"

"Nick and me."

"Can't I come?"

"Then we'd all three be locked out."

There was a long silence, and I thought maybe he'd decided just to forget it and go back to sleep.

"How long will you be gone?"

"Ten minutes," I told him. "At the most."

"Who you gonna see?"

"Magdalena," Nick told him.

R.X. cackled, and we all had to get quiet until we were sure Mr. Star was still asleep. That was easy, though. He slept loud.

"Okay," R.X. told me. "But hurry."

"If Quint and those guys call again, answer it fast," Nick told him.

"They've got a coach in there who's always on their backs. How come they can make midnight phone calls and we can't?" R.X. asked him.

"Got me," Nick said.

R.X. slumped down by the door as Nick and I sneaked out. The note and plastic ice cube were in my pocket, ready for delivery.

As I stepped into the hall I looked to the right and grabbed Nick's arm. Sitting on a tilted-back chair in front of the Pig guys' door was their coach. No way *they* were getting out. He wasn't looking our way. Actually, when we looked closer, we saw that he wasn't looking *any* way. His chin had dropped down to his chest. He was sound asleep.

If we turned right to get to the elevator we might wake him up, and he'd make us march back in to Mr. Star. Mr. Star would not wake up happy.

We'd never turned left before, but it was a big building, so left had to lead somewhere. Edging down the hall in our bare feet, we walked close to the wall until we turned the corner. Then we ran. Nobody yelled at us. We ran till we found steps to race down to the first floor.

That landed us by the game room. A metal gate was pulled across it, and it was locked. The game room, I remembered, was just down the hall from the W.O.R.M. room.

I remembered right. It was there, but it was empty. The signs, the people, and the three-foot trophy were gone.

"He said midnight?" Nick asked.

"It's what he said. The banquet must be someplace else."

We were the only kids in the hall. Most of the adult types were heading for the atrium. Somebody was playing music there, not live—some kind of weird recorded music. If R.X. was still awake he could hear it in our room.

"Let's check it out," I said. "Act like you belong." This wasn't easy. We were kids alone at midnight and everybody else had shoes on. Inside, the atrium was different than before, darker for one thing. There were red and blue spotlights near the pool and some round tables set up for eating.

I looked at my watch. It was ten minutes to midnight.

I didn't see Mr. Crook. These people just looked like ordinary people. No detective hats there, or clowns, either, that I could tell.

One thing was funny, though. Over on the far side of the pool where nobody was standing, the old ice seal was lying on a beach towel. It was a much thinner seal.

"Hey, look at *that,* will you?" Nick said. On one of the tables, a light shining straight at it, was the three-foot trophy. It gleamed. It looked as though you'd have to be the fastest, smartest person in the world to win it.

"I don't think I'd know the Crook man without

his hat. Do you see him anywhere?" Nick asked.

Nowhere. To stay out of the way, we wandered over to look at the seal. Though the lights weren't on it, it was shiny, too. I wondered why they'd saved it. Fiona said they'd got the seal for half price because it was going to do double duty.

"What's that in his head?" Nick asked. The ice was sparkling all over, but the left part of the seal's head was really glittery.

I bent over and gave it a close look. "I think I know what this means," I told Nick. "See this note?" I dug it out of my pocket. "On one side it's just the form the inspector uses to make his report. On the other side—"

"Hobie?" a voice said. "I *thought* it was you. Does your coach know you're here?" He put out his hand. "I think I remember this young man from earlier in the day."

"This is Nick," I told him, as they shook hands. "Actually, Mr. Star thinks we're asleep. If he finds out we're not there, he'll kill us."

"So to speak," he said, laughing. "Run along then."

"Yeah, but first we've got something for you."

I handed him the plastic ice cube. "This was in our room most of the afternoon, but I didn't know it."

He took the fake ice and frowned. You could tell it didn't mean anything to him.

"Somebody kicked it all the way from the third floor ice machine. And *this* paper was wrapped around it. See what it says on the back—S(T)EAL."

"When you take the T out of steal it says seal," Nick told us. He was beginning to get into this.

"Look at that seal," I said. "It's got sparkly stuff in its head. Is it what I think it is?"

Mr. Crook whipped a big magnifying glass out

of his pocket. "The grandchildren gave me this to bring along. It was part of my birthday present." He laughed. "They said no good detective could do without a magnifying glass, but I think they really got it to help me read the Sunday papers." Then he peered through it at the seal's head.

"Is the sparkly stuff what I think it is?" I asked him again. "Is it the necklace?"

"Ah-ha!" Mr. Crook straightened up and smiled. Then he leaned back over, glanced around to see if anybody was looking, and whispered, "The motel inspector was checking the ice machines. He found out somebody was stealing jewels, so the thief murdered him with a piece of poisoned chocolate cake!"

"The seal was a clue all along," I told him.

"This is beautiful," he said. "A thief was hiding ice—that's what criminals call precious stones, you know—ice. It's in *all* the jewel-robbery books. He was hiding ice in ice. Perfect."

"Do you know who was doing it?" Nick asked.

"Well," Mr. Crook said, "the note had to have been written by Vic Tim."

"That's the guy who was murdered," I explained to Nick. "Vic must have found the jewels."

"But who hid them in the seal? Who had him killed?" Mr. Crook looked over at the rest of the group gathered by the trophy. "Everybody here thinks it's either the motel owner or the motel manager because they threatened Vic Tim."

"Where did the chocolate cake come from?" Nick asked.

"The chef!" Mr. Crook and I said together.

"The chef did it!" I said.

"The splendid chef who served our club such a fine lunch. He's famous for carving ice, and he made the poison cake. We have to declare him the murderer."

"Why didn't Vic Tim just write 'the chef did it' on the paper?" Nick asked.

"Because then it wouldn't have been a mystery," I told him.

Mr. Crook sighed and put the paper and the round plastic ice cube in his pocket. "All the pieces fit! I thank you. My children thank you. My grandchildren thank you. They'll love this. How can I thank you enough?"

"By saving me from swimming pools every time I'm dressed up like a penguin," I told him.

"Listen, this has been more fun than elevator

tag," Nick said, "but we've got to go. We've really got to go." We shook hands with Mr. Crook, and then we ran. The fake grass tickled my feet.

Running was a mistake. "You! Boys!" It was the guy from security, working late. I couldn't tell if he knew I was the penguin or not. We ran faster than he did, back to the game room and up the steps. Without looking back, we rushed to the third floor and dashed down the hall.

But as we rounded the corner we saw that somebody was standing in front of our door. We couldn't go forward. We sure couldn't go back. The security guy might be looking on the second floor, or he might be right behind us.

It was Magdalena. You couldn't miss her. She was wearing a red flannel nightshirt. Her long brown pigtail flipped as she checked both ways to see if anyone was coming. Not only was she a head taller than me, but she had very quick reflexes. Mr. Star kept pointing that out during the video.

"I saw you sneak away," she whispered when we got there. "I thought probably you'd be back." She glanced behind her again. "Our coach woke up about two minutes after you left.

Nothing was happening, so he gave up and went to bed. That's when he caught the boys making phone calls. If you'd been standing in the hall you could have heard him shout at them. You're lucky he didn't catch you."

I rapped quietly on our door. "There's a guy downstairs who's after us now," I told her. "We haven't done anything wrong, though."

"You mean running up and down the halls at midnight is okay?" she asked.

"Well," Nick said, knocking again, "aside from that, we haven't done anything wrong."

"I just wanted to thank you before you went home," Magdalena said, and she smiled at me, "and to tell you that it was really nice of you to apologize like that."

"Apologize?" I didn't remember saying I was sorry for anything.

"I mean, after a guy from your team kicked mud in my face, your throwing me the roses." If she knew it was Nick who'd sprayed her she didn't let on. "That was very nice."

"You're welcome," I said. I figured why tell her it wasn't true? Anyway, I was glad she'd caught the flowers. Did it count when you did something right without meaning to?

Down the hall, a door slammed. Two girls ran from one room to another.

Nick leaned down and called through the crack under our door.

"Well, good luck tomorrow," I told her.

If Nick and I got caught, we wouldn't even *play* tomorrow. It always counts when you do something *wrong* without meaning to. I just forgot about the dentist. I didn't mean to ride through the cement. I didn't mean for the Jell-O and shrimp to splash into the pool. I didn't plan to be standing here in the hall with a girl at midnight.

A lock clicked close by. A knob turned. It was too late to run. There was no place to hide. I wondered if Toby would let me ride his Big Wheel to school when Dad took my bike away.

The door that opened was not ours. It was the one right next to ours, the girls' room. Lisa stuck her head out. She looked at us once. Then she looked again like she couldn't believe it.

"It's Ho-bie!" she yelped. "And Nick! And . . . Mudface! Molly," she called, "you're not going to believe this." And she slammed the door.

We'll never play soccer again, I thought. We're dead meat.

Nick turned our doorknob. "R.X.," he called. And again. "R.X."

Magdelena didn't panic. "I live a long way from here," she said, "but you can send me a letter if you want to." She handed me a piece of paper with her name and address on it. Then she walked back down the hall.

I stuck the note in my pocket with the pink rose. Nick and I looked at each other. He was too scared, I could tell, even to tease me. Through the door of the girls' room we could hear Molly and Lisa laughing like crazy. The other girls were laughing with them. They were shrieking. They were going to wake up the whole world laughing.

I was about to pound on our door, so at least we wouldn't get caught by the security man again, when suddenly Marshall opened it, rubbing his eyes.

"What's going on?" he asked. On the floor behind him R.X. was curled up sleeping. "Did I hear Lisa? Even over Mr. Star's snores, I thought I heard Lisa laughing." He blinked at us. "Wait a minute. You're all dressed. Have you been playing elevator tag without me?"

16. Maybe Next Year

It was two o'clock on Sunday afternoon before the van left the Megadome Motel for home. The day was sunny and warm. The game was over. The tournament was over. We were back on the open road.

"All right, now," Mrs. Rossi said. "Nobody asks 'When are we going to get there.' We'll get there when we get there. Promise?"

Everybody grumbled.

"I'm taking that as a promise," she said.

"Daring Devastators!" Molly groaned. She was

sitting in the front seat with Mrs. Rossi. Somehow Toby had talked his way into the back. Because we were very, very lucky, his car seat was now strapped between me and Nick.

"I still can't believe that team called themselves the Daring Devastators," Molly went on. "That's my name. I made it up. I *know* I made it up. And then they ruined it all by putting 'Dar Dev' on their shirts!"

"They weren't all that good, either," Lisa said. "You always said yours were good, Molly, except for those two, like, really bad players named Hunk and Dumdum. Were those two dwerps on their team named Hunk or Dumdum, did you ask?"

"This is no fair," Molly told us. "I have to change my whole story."

"Do one for me," Toby asked her. "I want a story for me. I want a story about a penguin who talks like Hobie."

"Penguins don't talk," Molly said. "If they did they certainly wouldn't sound like Hobie. Talking animals are in fantasies. I write true-to-life stories."

"I want a story," Toby said. "I want a story now."

It is not easy to argue with Toby. I know this from baby-sitting him. Either he wins or he cries. The van was too small for Toby's cries. "Okay," I said, "one short story coming up. Once upon a time there was a talking penguin—"

"Named Hobie," he said.

"This one was called Toby," I told him.

"Toby the Penguin," he said. "I like that."

"Toby was a very, very good penguin. He had a tiny car that he rode all day long. It was so tiny, he had to sit on the top of it. It was so tiny, it was the size of . . ."

". . . a banana," Toby said.

"It was as little as a banana," I agreed. "Every time he parked it at a parking meter, he slid off the front of the car that was big as a banana, and out popped . . ."

". . . out popped a hundred zillion clowns. They were all dressed up, and every time they popped out of his car they gave Toby the Penguin a big huge party with silver balloons and chocolate cake and licorice and they all lived happily ever after." He took a breath. "That was a good story," he said. "Tell me another one. Make Toby the Penguin win a soccer game."

"Later," I told him. "Much later."

"This trophy," Marshall said from the seat behind us, "is actually bigger than last year's trophy."

I turned and looked at it propped in the corner. The gold figure on top had his arms up high like he'd just won a race.

"And shinier, too," I told him.

"I bet it's three feet tall," Nick said. "Do you

think it'll fit in the Park District trophy case?"

"It says right here that this is the W.O.R.M award," R.X. told us. "That's gross. They won't put a worm prize in the trophy case. No way."

"I don't see why not," I said. "It doesn't have to be the same kind the Hot Shots had. They've got trophies in there for baseball and volleyball. There's even one for shuffleboard. I don't see why there couldn't be one for helping solve crime puzzles."

"Toby the Penguin is hungry," Toby said.

"That's because you didn't eat your lunch," I told him. "Here. I saved you a cracker."

He shook his head, clamped his mouth shut, and stared me down.

"This is a secret," I whispered in his ear. "Nobody knows this but you and me. What you see here is not a cracker, it's a crunchy stinkfish. Talking penguins love stinkfish."

"Eeeeeeuuuuu," he said and smiled. He took the cracker and licked it. Then he began to nibble. "Stinkfish are better than crackers," he said. "You got any more?"

I gave him one for each hand. When you baby-sit, you learn tricks like that to make kids happy. I had a feeling I was going to be needing lots more tricks over the next few months, enough to build two slabs of sidewalk.

"I still don't know how you did it," Lisa said. "I mean, like, I didn't even know there *was* a fake murder."

"No big deal. We just gave the man who won it a clue he couldn't find," Nick explained. "It was all pretty much luck."

"It was nothing," I said, looking back again to make sure the gold statue was still there.

"Mr. Star is behind us," Marshall said. "All the kids in his car are waving." We waved back. Mrs. Rossi beeped as they passed. R.X. pushed his nose up against the side window.

When Mr. Star went to check us out of the motel is when we got the trophy. Mr. Crook had left it with a message for him. Mr. Star gave the message to me. It said, "Two members of your Zapper team did a good deed for me." That made it sound as if we'd helped him cross a street. He didn't mention the penguin caper. I guess he figured that Mr. Star didn't really need to know.

Anyway, the note went on, "I'd like Hobie and

his friend Nick to have this trophy. Could you also give him this note of thanks."

Mr. Star tried to find out more, but Mr. Crook had already checked out of the Megadome. I explained about running into the W.O.R.M headquarters by mistake. I told him I had found the ice cube and note, but I didn't mention that we'd delivered them at midnight. I also left out the clown part. Mr. Star let us keep the trophy.

"I've started another draft," Molly called from the front seat. "My team will be named the Zappers, after all. They will win big."

"I think," Nick said, "I didn't make any goals this morning because I wasn't wearing my secret-pocket soccer shoes that slop mud in unsuspecting goalies' faces. All my sneakers did was sneak."

"Secretpocket soccershoes," Toby went, "secretpocket soccershoes," over and over and over.

"I didn't make a goal," Lisa said, "because I'm not a morning person."

"I didn't make a goal," R.X. said, "because I was so sleepy. Some girls in the room next to ours were screaming and giggling until practically dawn." Nick turned around and made him stop, so Mrs. Rossi wouldn't hear how the girls were also using their beds as trampolines and how we could hear them jumping until three o'clock. We'd figured if we didn't bug them about keeping us awake, they wouldn't tell about us talking to Magdelena at midnight. Mr. Star had snored through it all.

"I, personally, slept extremely well," Molly said. "But from what I hear—"

"Their second-half goalie seemed a little scared of us." I cut her off.

"A *lot* scared," Lisa said.

"That was Roscoe," Marshall explained. "Hobie drilled the ball right past him."

"One tiny goal," Molly said. "I think Roscoe had his eyes shut."

Roscoe was the kid we'd cornered playing elevator tag. He clearly thought Nick and Marshall and I were maniacs. I didn't see any real reason to change his mind, and so I bared my teeth and snarled when I drove in with the ball. It was true. He did close his eyes. I zapped the ball right in. Daring Devastators 0, Zappers 1.

We won. We won by one. It had a nice sound. I unfolded Mr. Crook's note to me and read it again.

Dear Hobie,

I'm grateful for your help in solving the (n)ice mystery. My children and grandchildren will, I know, be delighted with our adventures.

Earlier this year my dear wife Jane died. I had, for some months, been sitting in my room doing little but read mystery novels. My family wanted to break that lonely pattern. Thank you for helping.

By the way, I gave the motel a check to cover cleaning the pool of fruit salad and sausages and shrimp. I also presented a small sum from me and my "grandson" Hobie to the new bride and groom. We did, after all, attend their memorable wedding reception.

I'm looking to the future again. Next winter I will go to Florida and visit Klown Kollege. Do you think it's too late for me to start a new career?

Continued thanks, and very best regards,

Albert T. Crook III

The letter, I decided, was even better than the trophy.

"Guess what," Molly said. "I'm going to have

this story finished before we get home." She held up her notebook so we could see all the words she'd written. "What happens is that the Zappers win big. The snake sandwich was really tuna and the girl got well. And it turns out that the were-wolf bite was just made by a mosquito. What do you think?"

"So they all live happily ever after," Lisa said.

"Because one of them," Nick went on, "turned into a circus clown and found a seal with its head full of diamonds and won the heart of a fair maiden."

Molly turned and frowned.

Everybody else laughed, like that was one of those impossible fantasies Molly said she doesn't write. It wasn't a fantasy, though. I could prove it. I had this mashed pink rose and the address of an amazing goalie in my pocket.

"Hey, Cement-sicker," Nick said, "what are you gonna tell your dad about this trip?"

I'd been thinking about that. He'd be waiting for us, and Mr. Star would tell him about how we lost our first game, but how I'd made the winning goal in our last one. And then I'd tell him that, just like Mr. Star always said we should, I'd had a very good time. My nose—I rubbed it to make sure—was clean; not a spot of yellow on it.

Everything would be okay. I was going to have to spend a lot of time changing yucky diapers and chasing little kids and telling them stories. I was going to have to earn all that money, but I'd get to keep playing ball. I'd get to keep my bike. I would also have to keep it out of wet cement.

"No kidding," Nick said low in my ear. "Will you tell him what you did?"

I'll tell him later, I thought. Later I'll do it. In a couple of days I'll tell Mom and Dad about the swimming-pool soup and about Mr. Crook and the midnight ice. In a couple of days, maybe, we'll all think it's funny.

"Well, will you?" Nick asked, louder.

"Shhhhhhh," I whispered, pointing at Toby. "You'll wake him up." Toby the Penguin was fast asleep, a stinkfish cracker in his hand.

Jamie Gilson

and her husband, Jerry, travel a lot. On a trip to Kalamazoo, Michigan, they stayed in a motel where hundreds of fourth, fifth, and sixth grade soccer players were spending the night. The kids were in town for a weekend tournament. During the day they played soccer on the fields. Late at night they played soccer down the long narrow halls, with ice pucks from the ice-making machine. After hearing tales from the motel desk clerk, several coaches, and many players, Mrs. Gilson decided that out-of-town soccer was a most promising idea for a story.

The Gilsons live one block from the shores of Lake Michigan and one mile from Central School, which all three of their children attended. Because Mrs. Gilson had never watched a soccer game, Central School fifth graders taught her the rules. They also told her that a soccer game played in the mud is the best kind of soccer game. She believed them.

And that is how this book—her 14th—began.